CITY OF LIGHT

They came out from the shadow of a house into the level golden light. The sun lay, a molten blur, between the dark sea and the dark clouds, and the roofs of the City burned with unearthly fire. They stopped, looking into that tremendous brightness and darkness of the west. The sea wind, smelling of salt and space and wood smoke, blew cold in their faces.

"Don't you see," Lev said, "you can see it—you can see what it should be, what it is."

Luz saw it, with his eyes, she saw the glory, the City that should be, and was....

THE EYE OF THE HERON
a new novel by
URSULA K. LE GUIN
Award-Winning Author of
The Earthsea Trilogy

Other Bantam Books by Ursula K. Le Guin
Ask your bookseller for the books you have missed.

THE EYE OF THE HERON

Ursula K. Le Guin

BANTAM BOOKS

TORONTO • NEW YORK • LONDON • SYDNEY • AUCKLAND

THE EYE OF THE HERON
A Bantam Book / published by arrangement with
Harper & Row, Publishers, Inc.

PRINTING HISTORY
Harper & Row edition published January 1983
This work was originally published in *Millennial Women*,
edited by Virginia Kidd (Delacorte Press 1978).
Bantam edition / August 1984

ISBN 0-553-24258-X

Published simultaneously in the United States and Canada

PRINTED IN THE UNITED STATES OF AMERICA

H   0 9 8 7 6 5 4 3 2 1

THE EYE OF
THE HERON

1

In the sunlight in the center of a ring of trees Lev sat cross-legged, his head bent above his hands.

A small creature crouched in the warm, shallow cup of his palms. He was not holding it; it had decided or consented to be there. It looked like a little toad with wings. The wings, folded into a peak above its back, were dun-colored with shadowy streaks, and its body was shadow-colored. Three gold eyes like large pinheads adorned its head, one on each side and one in the center of the skull. This upward-looking central eye kept watch on Lev. Lev blinked. The creature changed. Dusty pinkish fronds sprouted out from under its folded wings. For a moment it appeared to be a feathery ball, hard to see clearly, for the fronds or feathers trembled continually, blurring its outlines. Gradually the blur died away. The toad with wings sat there as before, but now it was light blue. It scratched its left eye with the hindmost of its three left feet. Lev smiled. Toad, wings, eyes, legs vanished. A flat mothlike shape crouched on Lev's palm, almost invisible because it was, except for some shadowy patches, exactly the same color and texture as his skin. He sat motionless. Slowly the blue toad with wings reappeared, one golden eye keeping watch on him. It walked across his palm and up the curve of his fingers. The six tiny, warm feet gripped and released, delicate and precise. It paused on the tip of his fingers and cocked its head to look at him with its right eye while its left and central eyes scanned the sky. It gathered itself into an arrow shape, shot out two translucent underwings twice the length of its body, and flew off in a long effortless glide toward a sunlit slope beyond the ring of trees.

"Lev?"

"Entertaining a wotsit." He got up, and joined Andre outside the tree-ring.

"Martin thinks we might get home tonight."

"Hope he's right," Lev said. He picked up his back-pack and joined the end of the line of seven men. They set off in single file, not talking except when one down the line called to indicate to the leader a possible easier way to take, or when the second in line, carrying the compass, told the leader to bear right or left. Their direction was southwestward. The going was not hard, but there was no path and there were no landmarks. The trees of the forest grew in circles, twenty to sixty trees forming a ring around a clear central space. In the valleys of the rolling land the tree-rings grew so close, often interlocking, that the travelers' way was a constant alternation of forcing through undergrowth between dark shaggy trunks, clear going across spongy grass in the sunlit circle, then again shade, foliage, crowded stems and trunks. On the hillsides the rings grew farther apart, and sometimes there was a long view over winding valleys endlessly dappled with the soft rough red circles of the trees.

As the afternoon wore on a haze paled the sun. Clouds thickened from the west. A fine, small rain began to fall. It was mild, windless. The travelers' bare chests and shoulders shone as if oiled. Water-drops clung in their hair. They went on, bearing steadily south by west. The light grew grayer. In the valleys, in the circles of the trees, the air was misty and dark.

The lead man, Martin, topping a long stony rise of land, turned and called out. One by one they climbed up and stood beside him on the crest of the ridge. Below a broad river lay shining and colorless between dark beaches.

The eldest of them, Holdfast, got to the top last and stood looking down at the river with an expression of deep satisfaction. "Hullo there," he murmured, as to a friend.

"Which way to the boats?" asked the lad with the compass.

"Upstream," Martin said, tentative.

"Down," Lev proposed. "Isn't that the high point of the ridge, west there?"

They discussed it for a minute and decided to try downstream. For a little longer before they went on they stood in silence on the ridge top, from which they had a greater view of the world than they had had for many days. Across the river the forest rolled on southward in endless interlocking ring patterns under hanging clouds. Eastward, upriver, the land rose steeply; to the west the river wound in gray levels between lower hills. Where it disappeared from sight a faint brightness lay upon it, a hint of sunlight on the open sea. Northward, behind the travelers' backs, the forested hills, the days and miles of their journey, lay darkening into rain and night.

In all that immense, quiet landscape of hills, forest, river, no thread of smoke; no house; no road.

They turned west, following the spine of the ridge. After a kilometer or so the boy Welcome, in the lead now, hailed and pointed down to two black chips on the curve of a shingle beach, the boats they had pulled up there many weeks before.

They descended to the beach by sliding and scrambling down the steep ridge. Down by the river it seemed darker, and colder, though the rain had ceased.

"Dark soon. Should we camp?" Holdfast asked, in a reluctant tone.

They looked at the gray mass of the river sliding by, the gray sky above it.

"It'll be lighter out on the water," Andre said, pulling out the paddles from under one of the beached, overturned canoes.

A family of pouchbats had nested among the paddles. The half-grown youngsters hopped and scuttered off across the beach, squawking morosely, while the exasperated parents swooped after them. The men laughed, and swung the light canoes up to their shoulders.

They launched and set off, four to a boat. The paddles lifting caught the silver light of the west. Out in midstream the sky seemed lighter, and higher, the banks low and black on either hand.

> O when we come,
> O when we come to Lisboa,
> The white ships will be waiting,
> O when we come. . . .

One man in the first canoe began the song, two or three voices in the second picked it up. Around the brief, soft singing lay the silence of the wilderness, under and over it, before and after it.

The riverbanks grew lower, farther away, more shadowy. They were now on a silent flood of gray half a mile wide. The sky darkened between glance and glance. Then far to the south one point of light shone out, remote and clear, breaking the old dark.

Nobody was awake in the villages. They came up through the paddy fields, guided by their swinging lanterns. They smelled the heavy fragrance of peat-smoke in the air. They came quiet as the rain up the street between the little sleeping houses, until Welcome let out a yell: "Hey, we're home!" and flung open the door of his family's house. "Wake up, Mother! It's me!"

Within five minutes half the town was in the street. Lights were lit, doors stood open, children danced about, a hundred voices talked, shouted, questioned, welcomed, praised.

Lev went to meet Southwind as she came hurrying down the street, sleepy-eyed, smiling, a shawl drawn over her tangled hair. He put out his hands and took hers, stopping her. She looked up into his face and laughed. "You're back, you're back!"

Then her look changed; she glanced around very swiftly at the cheerful commotion of the street, and back at Lev.

"Oh," she said, "I knew it. I knew."

"On the way north. About ten days out. We were climbing down into a stream gorge. The rocks slipped under his hands. There was a nest of rock scorpions. He was all right at first. But there were dozens of stings. His hands began to swell. . . ."

His hands tightened on the girl's; she still looked into his eyes.

"He died in the night."

"In much pain?"

"No," Lev said, lying.

Tears filled his eyes.

"So he's there," he said. "We made a cairn of white boulders. Near a waterfall. So he—so he's there."

Behind them in the commotion and chatter a woman's voice sounded clearly: "But where's Timmo?"

Southwind's hands went loose in Lev's; she seemed to grow smaller, to shrink down, shrink away. "Come with me," he said, and they went in silence, his arm about her shoulders, to her mother's house.

Lev left her there with Timmo's mother and her own mother. He came out of the house and stood hesitant, then returned slowly toward the crowd. His father came forward to meet him; Lev saw the curly gray hair, the eyes seeking through torchlight. Sasha was a slight, short man; as they embraced Lev felt the bones beneath the skin, hard and frail.

"You were with Southwind?"

"Yes. I can't—"

He clung for a minute to his father, and the hard, thin hand stroked his arm. The torchlight blurred and stung in his eyes. When he let go, Sasha drew back to look at him, saying nothing, intent dark eyes, the mouth hidden by a bristly gray mustache.

"You've been all right, Father?"

Sasha nodded. "You're tired. Come on home." As they started down the street he said, "Did you find the promised land?"

"Yes. A valley. A river-valley. Five kilos from the sea. Everything we need. And beautiful—the mountains above it— Range behind range, higher and higher, higher than the clouds, whiter— You can't believe how high you have to look to see the highest peaks." He had stopped walking.

"Mountains in between? Rivers?"

Lev looked down from the white visionary heights, into his father's eyes.

"Enough to keep the Bosses from following us there?"

After a moment Lev smiled. "Maybe," he said.

* * *

It was the middle of the bog-rice harvest, so that many of the farming people could not come, but all the villages sent a man or woman to Shantih to hear what the explorers reported and what the people said. It was afternoon, still raining; the big open place in front of the Meeting House was crowded with umbrellas made of the broad, red, papery leaves of the thatch-tree. Under the umbrellas people stood or squatted on leaf-mats in the mud, and cracked nuts, and talked, until at last the little bronze bell of the Meeting House went *tonka-tonka-tonk*; then they all looked at the porch of the Meeting House, where Vera stood ready to speak.

She was a slender woman with iron-gray hair, a narrow nose, dark oval eyes. Her voice was strong and clear, and while she spoke there was no other sound but the quiet patter of the rain, and now and then the chirp of a little child in the crowd, quickly hushed.

She welcomed the explorers back. She spoke of Timmo's death, and, very quietly and briefly, of Timmo himself, as she had seen him on the day the exploring party left. She spoke of their hundred-day trek through the wilderness. They had mapped a great area east and north of Songe Bay, she said, and they had found what they went to find—a site for a new settlement, and a passable way to it. "A good many of us here," she said, "don't like the idea of a new settlement so far from Shantih. And among us now are also some of our neighbors from the City, who may wish to join in our plans and discussions. The whole matter must be fully considered and freely discussed.

So first let Andre and Lev speak for the explorers, and tell us what they saw and found."

Andre, a stocky, shy man of thirty, described their journey to the north. His voice was soft and he did not speak easily, but the crowd listened intently to his sketch of the world beyond their long-familiar fields. Some, towards the back, craned until they saw the men from the City, of whose presence Vera had politely warned them. There they were near the porch, six men in jerkins and high boots: Bosses' bodyguards, each with a long sheathed knife on the thigh and a whip, the thong neatly curled, tucked into the belt.

Andre mumbled to a close and gave place to Lev, a young man, slight and rawboned, with thick, black, bright hair. Lev also began hesitantly, groping for words to describe the valley they had found and why they thought it most suitable for settlement. As he spoke his voice warmed and he began to forget himself, as if he saw before him what he described: the wide valley and the river which they had named Serene, the lake above it, the bog-lands where rice grew wild, the forests of good timber, the sunny slopes where orchards and root crops could be planted and houses could stand free of the mud and damp. He told of the river mouth, a bay full of shellfish and edible kelp; and he spoke of the mountains that stood above the valley to the north and east, protecting it from the winds that made the winter a weariness of mud and cold at Songe. "The peaks of them go up and up into the silence and sunlight above the clouds," he said. "They shelter the valley, like a mother with a child in her arms. We called them the Mountains of the Mahatma. It was to see if the mountains kept off the storms that we stayed so long there, fifteen days. Early autumn there is like midsummer here, only the nights are colder; the days were sunny, and no rain. Holdfast thought there might be three rice harvests a year there. There's a good deal of fruit in the forests, and the fishing in the river and the bay shores would help feed the first year's settlers till the first harvest. The mornings are so bright there! It wasn't just to see how the weather was that we stayed. It was hard to leave the place, even to come home."

They listened with enchantment, and were silent when he stopped.

Somebody called, "How far is it, in days of travel?"

"Martin's guess is about twenty days, with families and big pack loads."

"Are there rivers to cross, dangerous places?"

"The best arrangement would be an advance party, a couple of days ahead, to mark out the easiest route. Coming back we avoided all the rough country we went through going north. The only difficult river crossing is right here, the Songe, that'll have to be done with boats. The others can be forded, till you get to the Serene."

More questions were shouted out; the crowd lost its enraptured quiet and was breaking into a hundred voluble discussions under the red-leaf umbrellas, when Vera came forward again and asked for silence. "One of our neighbors is here and wishes to talk with us," she said, and stood aside to let a man behind her come forward. He wore black, with a broad silver-embossed belt. The six men who had stood near the porch had come up on it with him and moved forward in a semicircle, separating him from the other people on the porch.

"Greetings to you all," the man in black said. His voice was dry, not loud.

"Falco," people murmured to one another. "The Boss Falco."

"I am pleased to present the congratulations of the Government of Victoria to these brave explorers. Their maps and reports will be a most valued addition to the Archives of the State in Victoria City. Plans for a limited migration of farmers and manual workers are being studied by the Council. Planning and control are necessary to ensure the safety and welfare of the community as a whole. As this expedition makes clear, we dwell in one corner, one safe haven, of a great and unknown world. We who have lived here longest, who keep the records of the early years of the Settlement, know that rash schemes of dispersal may threaten our survival, and that wisdom lies in order and strict cooperation. I am pleased to tell you that the Council will receive these brave explorers with the welcome of the City, and present them a suitable reward for their endeavors."

There was a different kind of silence.

Vera spoke; she looked fragile beside the group of bulky men, and her voice sounded light and clear. "We thank the representative of the Council for his courteous invitation."

Falco said, "The Council will expect to receive the explorers, and examine their maps and reports, in three days' time."

Again the pent silence.

"We thank Councillor Falco," Lev said, "and decline his invitation."

An older man tugged at Lev's arm, whispering hard; there was much quick, low talk among the people on the porch, but the crowd before the Meeting House kept silent and motionless.

"We must arrive at decisions on several matters," Vera said to Falco, but loud enough that all could hear, "before we're ready to reply to the invitation of the Council."

"The decisions have been made, Senhora Adelson. They have been made by the Council. Only your obedience is expected." Falco bowed, to her, raised his hand in salutation to the crowd, and left the porch, surrounded by his guards. The people moved wide apart to let them pass.

On the porch, two groups formed: the explorers and other men and women, mostly young, around Vera, and a larger group around a fair, blue-eyed man named Elia. Down among the crowd this pattern was repeated, until it began to look like a ringtree forest: small circles, mostly young, and larger circles, mostly older. All of them argued passionately, yet without anger. When one tall old woman began shaking her red-leaf umbrella at a vehement girl and shouting, "Runaway! You want to run away and leave us to face the Bosses! What you need is a spanking!"—with a whack of the umbrella in demonstration—then very rapidly the people around her seemed to melt away, taking with them the girl who had annoyed her. The old woman was left standing alone, as red as her umbrella, brandishing it sullenly at nothing. Presently, frowning and working her lips, she joined the outskirts of another circle.

The two groups up on the porch had now joined. Elia spoke with quiet intensity: "Direct defiance is violence, Lev, as much as any blow of fist or knife."

"As I refuse violence, I refuse to serve the violent," the young man said.

"If you defy the Council's request, you will cause violence."

"Jailings, beatings maybe; all right. Is it liberty we want, Elia, or mere safety?"

"By defying Falco, in the name of liberty or anything else, you provoke repression. You play into his hands."

"We're in his hands already, aren't we?" Vera said. "What we want is to get out."

"We all agree that it's time, high time, that we talk with the Council—talk firmly, reasonably. But if we begin with defiance, with moral violence, nothing will be achieved, and they'll fall back on force."

"We don't intend defiance," Vera said, "we shall simply hold fast to the truth. But if *they* begin with force, you know, Elia, even our attempt at reason becomes a resistance."

"Resistance is hopeless, we must *talk* together! If violence enters in, in act or word, the truth is lost— our life in Shantih, our liberty will be destroyed. Force will rule, as it did on Earth!"

"It didn't rule everybody on Earth, Elia. Only those who consented to serve it."

"Earth cast our fathers out," Lev said. There was a

brightness in his face; his voice caught at a harsh, yearning note, like the deep strings of a harp plucked hard. "We're outcasts, the children of outcasts. Didn't the Founder say that the outcast is the free soul, the child of God? Our life here in Shantih is not a free life. In the north, in the new settlement, we will be free."

"What is freedom?" said a beautiful, dark woman, Jewel, who stood beside Elia. "I don't think you come to it by the path of defiance, resistance, refusal. Freedom comes with you if you walk the path of love. To accept all is to be given all."

"We've been given a whole world," Andre said in his subdued voice. "Have we accepted it?"

"Defiance is a trap, violence is a trap, they must be refused—and that's what we're doing," Lev said. "We are going free. The Bosses will try to stop us. They'll use moral force, they may use physical force; force is the weapon of the weak. But if we trust ourselves, our purpose, our strength, if we hold fast, all their power over us will melt away like shadows when the sun comes up!"

"Lev," the dark woman said softly, "Lev, this is the world of shadows."

2

Rainclouds moved in long dim lines above Songe Bay. Rain pattered and pattered on the tile roof of the House of Falco. At the end of the house, in the kitchens, there was a far-off sound of life astir, of servants' voices. No other sound, no other voice, only the rain.

Luz Marina Falco Cooper sat in the deep window seat, her knees drawn up to her chin. Sometimes she gazed out through the thick, greenish glass of the window at the sea and the rain and the clouds. Sometimes she looked down at the book that lay open beside her, and read a few lines. Then she sighed and looked out the window again. The book was not interesting.

It was too bad. She had had high hopes of it. She had never read a book before.

She had learned to read and write, of course, being the daughter of a Boss. Besides memorizing lessons aloud, she had copied out moral precepts, and could write a letter offering or declining an invitation, with a fancy scrollwork frame, and the salutation and signature written particularly large and stiff. But at school they used slates and the copybooks which the schoolmistresses wrote out by hand. She had never touched a book. Books were too precious to be used in school; there were only a few dozen of them in the world. They were kept in the Archives. But, coming into the hall this afternoon, she had seen lying on the low table a little brown box; she had lifted the lid to see what was in it, and it was full of words. Neat, tiny words, all the letters alike, what patience to make them all the same size like that! A book—a real book, from Earth. Her father must have left it there. She seized it, carried it to the window seat, opened the

lid again carefully, and very slowly read all the
different kinds of words on the first leaf of paper.

FIRST AID

A MANUAL OF EMERGENCY CARE
FOR INJURIES AND ILLNESS

M. E. Roy, M.D.

The Geneva Press
Geneva, Switzerland
2027

License No. 83A38014
Gen.

It did not seem to make much sense. "First aid"
was all right, but the next line was a puzzle. It began
with somebody's name, A. Manuel, and then went on
about injuries. Then came a lot of capital letters with
dots after them. And what was a geneva, or a press,
or a switzerland?

Equally puzzling were the red letters which slanted
up the page as if they had been written over the
others: DONATED BY THE WORLD RED CROSS FOR THE USE
OF THE PENAL COLONY ON VICTORIA.

She turned the leaf of paper, admiring it. It was
smoother to the touch than the finest cloth, crisp yet
pliable like fresh thatch-leaf, and pure white.

She worked her way word by word to the bottom of
the first page, and then began to turn several pages
at once, since more than half the words meant nothing

anyway. Gruesome pictures appeared: her interest revived with a shock. People supporting other people's heads, breathing into their mouths; pictures of the bones inside a leg, of the veins inside an arm; colored pictures, on marvelous shiny paper like glass, of people with little red spots on their shoulders, with big red blotches on their cheeks, with horrible boils all over them, and mysterious words beneath the pictures: *Allergic Rash. Measles. Chicken Box. Small Box.* No, it was *pox*, not *box*. She studied all the pictures, sometimes making a foray into the words on the facing pages. She understood that it was a book of medicine, and that the doctor, not her father, must have left it on the table the night before. The doctor was a good man, but touchy; would he be angry if he knew she had looked at his book? It had his secrets in it. He never answered questions. He liked to keep his secrets to himself.

Luz sighed again and looked out at the ragged, rain-dropping clouds. She had looked at all the pictures, and the words were not interesting.

She got up, and was just setting the book down on the table exactly where it had lain, when her father entered the room.

His step was energetic, his back straight, his eyes clear and stern. He smiled when he saw Luz. A little startled, guilty, she swept him a fancy curtsy, her skirts hiding the table and the book. "Senhor! A thousand greetings!"

"There's my little beauty. Michael! Hot water and a towel! —I feel dirty all over." He sat down in one of the carved wooden armchairs and stretched out his legs, though his back stayed as straight as ever.

"Where have you been getting dirty, Papa?"

"Among the vermin."

"Shanty Town?"

"Three kinds of creature came from Earth to Victoria: Men, lice, and Shanty-Towners. If I could get rid of only one kind, it would be the last." He smiled again, pleased by his joke, then looked up at his daughter and said, "One of them presumed to answer me. I think you knew him."

"I knew him?"

"At school. Vermin shouldn't be allowed into the school. I forget his name. Their names are all nonsense, Sticktight, Holdfast, Howd'youdo, what have you. . . . A little black-haired stick of a boy."

"Lev?"

"That's the one. A troublemaker."

"What did he say to you?"

"He said no to me."

Falco's man came hurrying in with a pottery basin and a jug of steaming water; a maid followed with towels. Falco scrubbed his face and hands, puffing and blowing and talking through the water and the towels. "He and some others just came back from an expedition up north, into the wilderness. He claims they found a fine town site. They want the whole lot to move there."

"To leave Shanty Town? All of them?"

Falco snorted in assent, and stuck out his feet for Michael to take off his boots. "As if they'd last one winter without the City to look after them! Earth sent them here fifty years ago as unteachable imbeciles, which is what they are. It's time they relearned their lesson."

"But they can't just go off into the wilderness," said Luz, who had been listening to her thoughts as well as to her father's words. "Who'd farm our fields?"

Her father ignored her question by repeating it, thus transforming a feminine expression of emotion into a masculine assessment of fact. "They can't, of course, be allowed to start scattering like this. They provide necessary labor."

"Why is it that Shanty-Towners do almost all the farming?"

"Because they're good for nothing else. Get that slop out of the way, Michael."

"Hardly any of our people know how to farm," Luz observed. She was thinking. She had dark, strongly arched eyebrows, as her father did, and when she was thinking they lay in a straight line above her eyes. This straight line displeased her father. It did not suit the face of a pretty girl of twenty. It gave her a hard, unwomanly look. He had often told her this, but she had never broken the bad habit.

"My dear, we are City people, not peasants."

"But who did the farming before the Shanty-Towners came? The Colony was sixty years old when they came."

"The working people did the manual work, of course. But even our working people were never peasants. We are City people."

"And we starved, didn't we? There were the

Famines." Luz spoke dreamily, as if recalling an old history recitation, but her eyebrows were still down in that straight black line. "In the first ten years of the Colony, and other times . . . lots of people starved. They didn't know how to cultivate bog-rice or raise sugar-root, until the Shanty-Towners came."

Her father's black brows were now a straight line too. He dismissed Michael, the maid, and the subject of conversation with one wave of the hand. "It's a mistake," he said in his dry voice, "to send peasants and women to school. The peasants become insolent, the women become boring."

It would have made her cry, two or three years ago. She would have wilted, and crept off to her room to weep, and been miserable until her father said something kind to her. But these days he could not make her cry. She didn't know why it was, and it seemed very strange to her. Certainly she feared and admired him as much as ever; but she always knew what he was going to say. It was never anything new. Nothing was ever new.

She turned and looked out through the thick, whorled glass again at Songe Bay, the farther curve of the shore veiled by unending rain. She stood straight, a vivid figure in the dull light, in her long red homespun skirt and ruffled shirt. She looked indifferent, and alone, standing there in the center of the high, long room; and she felt so. Also she felt her father's gaze on her. And knew what he was going to say.

"It's time you were married, Luz Marina."

She waited for the next sentence.

"Since your mother died. . . ." And the sigh.

Enough, enough, enough!

She turned to face him. "I read that book," she said.

"Book?"

"Doctor Martin must have left it. What does it mean, 'penal colony'?"

"You had no business to touch that!"

He was surprised. That at least made things interesting.

"I thought it was a box of dried fruits," she said, and laughed. "But what does it mean, 'penal colony'? A colony of criminals, a prison?"

"That is nothing you need to know."

"Our ancestors were sent here as prisoners, is that right? That's what the Shanty-Towners in school said." Falco's face was getting white, but the danger exhilarated Luz; her mind raced, and she spoke her mind. "They said the First Generation were all criminals. The Earth Government used Victoria for a jail. The Shanty-Towners said *they* were sent because they believed in peace or something, but *we* were sent because we were all thieves and murderers. And most of them, the First Generation, were men, their women couldn't come unless they were married to them, and that's why there were so few women to start with. That always seemed stupid, not to send enough women for a colony. And it explains why the ships were made only to come, not to go back. And why the Earth people never come here. We're locked out. It's true, isn't it? We call ourselves Victoria Colony. But we're a jail."

Falco had risen. He came forward; she stood still,

poised on her feet. "No," she said, lightly, as if indifferent. "No, don't, Papa."

Her voice stopped the man in his anger; he too
stood still, and looked at her. For a moment he saw
her. She saw in his eyes that he saw her, and that he
was afraid. For a moment, only a moment.

He turned away. He went to the table and picked
up the book Dr. Martin had left. "What does all that
matter, Luz Marina?" he said at last.

"I'd like to know."

"It was a hundred years ago. And Earth is lost. And
we are what we are."

She nodded. When he spoke that way, dry and
quiet, she saw the strength she admired and loved in
him.

"What angers me," he said, but not with anger, "is
that you listened to that talk from those vermin. They
put everything backward. What do they know? You
let them tell you that Luis Firmin Falco, my great-
grandfather, the founder of our House, was a thief, a
jailbird. What do they know about it! I know, and I
can tell you, what our ancestors were. They were men.
Men too strong for Earth. The Government on Earth
sent them here because they were afraid of them. The
best, the bravest, the strongest—all the thousands of
little weak people on Earth were afraid of them, and
trapped them, and sent them off in the one-way ships,
so that they could do as they liked with Earth, you
see. Well, when that was done, when the real men
were gone, the Earth people were left so weak and
womanish that they began to be afraid even of rabble
like the Shanty-Towners. So they sent them here for

us to keep in order. Which we have done. You see? That's how it was."

Luz nodded. She accepted her father's evident intent to placate her, though she did not know why for the first time he had spoken to her placatingly, explaining something as if she were his equal. Whatever the reason, his explanation sounded well; and she was used to hearing what sounded well, and figuring out later what it might really mean. Indeed, until she had met Lev at school, it had not occurred to her that anyone might prefer to speak a plain fact rather than a lie that sounded well. People said what suited their purposes, when they were serious; and when they weren't serious, they talked without meaning anything at all. Talking to girls, they were hardly ever serious. Ugly truths were to be kept from girls, so that their pure souls did not become coarse and soiled. And anyhow, she had asked about the penal colony mostly to get her father off the subject of her marriage; and the trick had worked.

But the trouble with such tricks, she thought when she was in her own room alone, is that they trick you too. She had tricked herself into arguing with her father, and winning the argument. He would not forgive her that.

All the girls of her age and class in the City had been married for two or three years now. She had evaded marriage only because Falco, whether he knew it or not, didn't want to let her go from his house. He was used to having her there. They were alike, very much alike; they enjoyed each other's company more, perhaps, than anyone else's. But he had looked at her this evening as if seeing someone different, someone he wasn't used to. If he began noticing her as a person different from himself, if she began winning battles with him, if she was no longer his little girl pet, he might begin thinking about what else she was—what use she was.

And what use was she, what was she good for? The continuation of the house of Falco, of course. And then what? Either Herman Marquez or Herman Macmilan. And nothing whatever she could do about it. She would be a wife. She would be a daughter-in-law. She would wear her hair in a bun, and scold the servants, and listen to the men carousing in the hall after supper, and have babies. One a year. Little Marquez Falcos. Little Macmilan Falcos. Eva, her old playmate, married at sixteen, had three babies and was expecting the fourth. Eva's husband, the Councillor's son Aldo Di Giulio Hertz, beat her; and she was proud of it. She showed the bruises and murmured, "Aldito has such a temper, he's so wild, like a little boy in a tantrum."

Luz made a face, and spat. She spat on the tiled floor of her room, and let the spittle lie. She stared at the small grayish blob and wished she could drown Herman Marquez in it, and then Herman Macmilan. She felt dirty. Her room was close, dirty: a prison cell. She fled the thought, and the room. She darted out into the hall, gathered up her skirts, and climbed the ladder to the place under the roof, where nobody else ever came. She sat on the dusty floor there—the roof, loud with rain, was too low to stand up under —and let her mind go free.

It went straight out, away from the house and the hour, back to a wider time.

On the playing field by the schoolhouse, an afternoon of spring, two boys were playing catch, Shanty-Towners, Lev and his friend Timmo. She stood on the porch of the schoolhouse watching them, wondering at what she saw, the reach and stretch of back and arm, the lithe swing of the body, the leap of the ball through light. It was as if they played a silent music, the music of moving. The light came under storm clouds, from the west, over Songe Bay, level and golden; the earth was brighter than the sky. The bank of raw earth behind the field was golden, the weeds above it burned. The earth burned. Lev stood waiting to catch a long throw, his head back, his hands poised, and she stood watching, amazed by beauty.

A group of City boys came around the schoolhouse to play football. They yelled at Lev to hand over the ball, just as he leaped, his arm at full stretch, to catch Timmo's high throw. He caught it, and laughed, and tossed the ball over to the others.

As the two came by the porch, she ran down the steps. "Lev!"

The west blazed behind him, he stood black between her and the sun.

"Why did you give them the ball like that?"

She could not see his face against the light. Timmo, a tall, handsome boy, held back a little and did not look into her face.

"Why do you let them push you around?"

Lev answered at last. "I don't," he said. As she came closer to him she saw him looking straight at her.

"They say 'Give it here!' And you just give it—"

"They want to play a game; we were just fooling around. We had our turn."

"But they don't ask you for it, they order you. Don't you have any pride?"

Lev's eyes were dark, his face was dark and rough, unfinished; he smiled, a sweet, startled smile. "Pride? Sure. If I didn't, I'd hang onto it when it's their turn."

"Why are you always so full of answers?"

"Because life's so full of questions."

He laughed, but he kept looking at her as if she were a question herself, a sudden question with no answer. And he was right, for she had no idea why she was challenging him like this.

Timmo stood by, a little uncomfortable. Some of the boys on the playing field were already looking at them: two Shanty-boys talking to a senhorita.

Without a word said, the three walked away from the schoolhouse, down to the street below it, where they could not be seen from the field.

"If any of them talked to each other like that, the way they yelled at you," Luz said, "there'd have been a fight. Why don't you fight?"

"For a football?"

"For anything!"

"We do."

"When? How? You just walk away."

"We walk into the City, to school, every day," Lev said. He was not looking at her now as they walked along side by side, and his face looked as usual, an ordinary boy's face, stubborn, sullen. She did not understand what he meant at first, and when she did, she did not know what to say.

"Fists and knives are the least of it," he said, and perhaps heard pomposity in his own voice, a certain boastfulness, for he turned to Luz with a laugh and shrug—"and words aren't much good either!"

They came out from the shadow of a house into the level golden light. The sun lay, a molten blur, between the dark sea and the dark clouds, and the roofs of the City burned with unearthly fire. The three young people stopped, looking into that tremendous brightness and darkness of the west. The sea wind, smelling of salt and space and wood smoke, blew cold in their faces. "Don't you see," Lev said, "you can see it—you can see what it should be, what it is."

She saw it, with his eyes, she saw the glory, the City that should be, and was.

The moment broke. The haze of glory still burned between sea and storm, the City still stood golden and endangered on the eternal shore; but people came down the street behind them, talking and calling. They were Shanty-girls, who had stayed in school to help the mistresses clean up the classrooms. They joined Timmo and Lev, greeting Luz gently but, like Timmo, warily. Her way home lay to the left, down into the City; theirs to the right, up over the bluffs and onto the Town Road.

As she went down the steep street she glanced back at them going up it. The girls wore work suits of bright, soft colors. City girls sneered at Shanty girls for wearing trousers; but they made their own skirts of Shanty cloth if they could get it, for it was finer and better dyed than any the City made. The boys' trousers and long-sleeved, high-necked jackets were the creamy white of the natural silkweed fiber. Lev's head of thick, soft hair looked very black above that whiteness. He was walking behind the others, with Southwind, a beautiful, low-voiced girl. Luz could tell from the way his head was turned that he was listening to that low voice, and smiling.

"Screw!" said Luz, and strode down the street, her long skirts whipping at her ankles. She had been too well brought up to know swearwords. She knew "Hell!" because her father said it, even in front of women, when he was annoyed. She never said "Hell!" —it was her father's property. But Eva had told her, years ago, that "screw" was a very bad word, and so, when alone, she used it.

And there, materializing like a wotsit out of nothing, and like a wotsit humpbacked, beady-eyed, and vaguely feathery, there was her duenna, Cousin Lores, who she thought had given up and gone home half an hour ago. "Luz Marina! Luz Marina! Where were you? I waited and waited—I ran all the way to Casa Falco and back to the school—where were you? Why are you walking all by yourself? Slow down, Luz Marina, I'm dying, I'm dying."

But Luz would not slow down for the poor squawking woman. She strode on, fighting tears that had come upon her unawares: tears of anger because she could never walk alone, never do anything by herself, never. Because the men ran everything. They had it all their way. And the older women were all on their side. So that a girl couldn't walk in the streets of the City alone, because some drunken working man might insult her, and what if he did get put in jail or get his ears cut off for it afterward? A lot of good that would do. The girl's reputation would be ruined. Because her reputation was what the men thought of her. The men thought everything, did everything, ran everything, made everything, made the laws, broke the laws, punished the lawbreakers; and there was no room left for the women, no City for the women. Nowhere, nowhere, but in their own rooms, alone.

Even a Shanty-Towner was freer than she was. Even Lev, who wouldn't fight for a football, but who challenged the night as it came up over the edge of the world, and laughed at the laws. Even Southwind, who was so quiet and mild—Southwind could walk home with anyone she liked, hand in hand across the open fields in the wind of evening, running before the rain.

The rain drummed on the tile roof of the attic, where she had taken refuge that day three years ago when she got home at last, Cousin Lores puffing and squawking behind her all the way.

The rain drummed on the tile roof of the attic, where she had taken refuge today.

Three years, since that evening in the golden light. And nothing to show for it. Less now than there had been then. Three years ago she had still gone to school; she had believed that when school was over she would magically be free.

A prison. All Victoria was a prison, a jailhouse. And no way out. Nowhere else to go.

Only Lev had gone away, and found a new place somewhere far in the north, in the wilderness, a place to go. . . . And he had come back from it, and had stood up and said "No" to the Boss Falco.

But Lev was free, he had always been free. That was why there was no other time in her life, before or since, like the time when she had stood with him on the heights of her City in the golden light before the storm, and seen with him what freedom was. For one moment. A gust of the sea wind, a meeting of the eyes.

It was more than a year since she had even seen him. He was gone, back to Shanty Town, off to the new settlement, gone free, forgetting her. Why should he remember her? Why should she remember him? She had other things to think about. She was a grown woman. She had to face life. Even if all life had to show her was a locked door, and behind the locked door, no room.

3

The two human settlements on the planet Victoria were six kilometers apart. There were, so far as the inhabitants of Shantih Town and Victoria City knew, no others.

A good many people had work, hauling produce or drying fish, which took them from one settlement to the other frequently, but there were many more who lived in the City and never went to the Town, or who lived in one of the farm-villages near the Town and never from year's end to year's end went to the City.

As a small group, four men and a woman, came down the Town Road to the edge of the bluffs, several of them looked with lively curiosity and considerable awe at the City spread out beneath them on the hilly shore of Songe Bay; they stopped just under the Monument Tower—the ceramic shell of one of the ships that had brought the first settlers to Victoria—but did not spend much time looking up at it; it was a familiar sight, impressive by its size, but skeletal and rather pitiful set up there on the cliff-top, pointing bravely at the stars but serving merely as a guide to fishing boats out at sea. It was dead; the City was alive. "Look at that," said Hari, the eldest of the group. "You couldn't count all those houses if you sat here for an hour! Hundreds of them!"

"Just like a city on Earth," another, a more frequent visitor, said with proprietary pride.

"My mother was born in Moskva, in Russia the Black," a third man said. "She said the City would only be a little town, there on Earth." But this was rather farfetched, to people whose lives had been spent between the wet fields and the huddled villages, in a close continuous bind of hard work and human companionship, outside which lay the immense, indifferent wilderness. "Surely," one of them said with mild disbelief, "she meant a big town?" And they stood beneath the hollow shell of the space ship, looking at the bright rust color of the tiled and thatched roofs, and the smoking chimneys, and the geometrical lines of walls and streets, and not looking at the vast landscape of beaches and bay and ocean, empty valleys, empty hills, empty sky, that surrounded the City with a tremendous desolation.

Once they came down past the schoolhouse into the streets they could entirely forget the presence of the wilderness. They were surrounded on all sides by the works of mankind. The houses, mostly row-built, lined the way on both sides with high walls and little windows. The streets were narrow, and a foot deep in mud. In places walkways of planking were laid over the mud, but these were in bad repair, and slippery with rain. Few people passed, but an open door might give a glimpse into the swarming interior courtyard of a house, full of women, washing, children, smoke, and voices. Then again the cramped, sinister silence of the street.

"Wonderful! Wonderful!" sighed Hari.

They passed the factory where iron from the Government mines and foundry was made into tools, kitchenware, door latches, and so on. The doorway was wide open, and they stopped and peered into the sulfurous darkness lit with sparking fires and loud with banging and hammering, but a workman yelled at them to move on. So they went on down to Bay Street, and looking at the length and width and straightness of Bay Street, Hari said again, "Wonderful!" They followed Vera, who knew her way about the City, up Bay Street to the Capitol. At the sight of the Capitol, Hari had no words left, but merely stared.

It was the biggest building in the world—four times the height of any common house—and built of solid stone. Its high porch was supported by four columns, each a single huge ringtree trunk, grooved and whitewashed, the heavy capitals carved and gilt. The visitors felt small passing between these columns, small entering the portals that gaped so wide and tall. The entry hall, narrow but also very high, had plastered walls, and these had been decorated years ago with frescoes that stretched from floor to ceiling. At the sight of these the people from Shantih stopped again and gazed, silent; for they were pictures of the Earth.

There were still people in Shantih who remembered Earth and would tell about it, but the memories, fifty-five years old, were mostly of things seen by children. Few were left who had been adults at the time of the exile. Some had spent years of their lives in writing down the history of the People of the Peace and the sayings of its leaders and heroes, and descriptions of the Earth, and sketches of its remote, appalling history. Others had seldom spoken of the Earth; at most they had sung to their children born in exile, or to their children's children, an old song with strange names and words in it, or told them tales about the children and the witch, the three bears, the king who rode on a tiger. The children listened round-eyed. "What is a bear? Does a king have stripes too?"

The first generation of the City, on the other hand, sent to Victoria fifty years before the People of the Peace, had mostly come from the cities, Buenos Aires, Rio, Brasilia, and the other great centers of Brasil-America; and some of them had been powerful men, familiar with stranger things even than witches and bears. So the fresco painter had painted scenes that were entirely marvelous to the people now looking at them: towers full of windows, streets full of wheeled machines, skies full of winged machines; women with shimmering, bejeweled clothes and blood-red mouths; men, tall heroic figures, doing incredible things— sitting on huge four-legged beasts or behind big shiny blocks of wood, shouting with arms upraised at vast crowds of people, advancing among dead bodies and pools of blood at the head of rows of men all dressed alike, under a sky full of smoke and bursting fire. . . . The visitors from Shantih must either stand there gazing for a week in order to see it all, or hurry on past at once, because they should not be late to the Council meeting. But they all stopped once more at the last panel, which was different from the others. Instead of being filled with faces and fire and blood and machines, it was black. Low in the left corner was a little blue-green disk, and high in the right corner was another; between and around them, nothing—black. Only if you looked close at the blackness did you see that it was flecked with a countless minute glittering of stars; and at last you saw the finely drawn silver space ship, no longer than a fingernail-paring, poised in the void between the worlds.

At the doorway beyond the black fresco two guards stood, imposing figures, dressed alike in wide trousers, jerkins, boots, belts. They carried not only coiled whips stuck in their belts, but guns: long muskets, with hand-carved stocks and heavy barrels. Most of the Shantih people had heard of guns but never seen one, and they stared with curiosity at them.

"Halt!" said one of the guards.

"What?" said Hari. The people of Shantih had early adopted the language spoken in Victoria City, since they had been people of many different tongues and needed a common language among themselves and with the City; but some of the older ones had not learned some of the City usages. Hari had never heard the word "Halt."

"Stop there," the guard said.

"All right," Hari said. "We're to wait here," he explained to the others.

The sound of voices making speeches came from behind the closed doors of the Council Room. The Shantih people presently began to wander back down the hall to look at the frescoes while they waited; the guards ordered them to wait in a group, and they came wandering back. At last the doors were opened, and the delegation from Shantih was escorted by the guards into the Council Hall of the Government of Victoria: a big room, filled with grayish light from windows set up high in the wall. At the far end was a raised platform on which ten chairs stood in a half-circle; on the wall behind them hung a sheet of red cloth, with a blue disk in the middle, and ten yellow stars around the disk. A couple of dozen men sat here and there on the rows of benches, facing the dais. Of the ten chairs on the dais, only three were occupied.

A curly-headed man who sat by a little table just below the dais stood up and announced that a delegation from Shanty Town had asked permission to address the Supreme Plenum of the Congress and Council of Victoria.

"Permission granted," said one of the men on the dais.

"Come forward—no, not there, along the side—" The curly man whispered and fussed till he got the delegation where he wanted them, near the platform. "Who is the spokesman?"

"Her," said Hari, nodding at Vera.

"State your name as listed in the National Registry. You are to address the Congressmen as 'Gentlemen' and the Councillors as 'Your Excellencies,'" the clerk whispered, frowning with agitation. Hari watched him with benign amusement, as if he were a pouchbat. "Go on, go on!" the clerk whispered, sweating.

Vera took a step forward from the group. "I'm Vera Adelson. We came to discuss with you our plans for sending a group north to start a new settlement. We hadn't had time the other day to talk the matter over, and so there was some misunderstanding and disagreement. That's all settled. Jan has the map that Councillor Falco asked for, we're happy to give you this copy for the Archives. The explorers warn us that it's not very accurate, but it does give a general idea of the country north and east of Songe Bay, including some passable routes and fords. We cordially hope that it may be of use to our community." One of the men held out a roll of leafpaper, and the worried clerk took it, glancing up at the Councillors for permission.

Vera, in her trouser-suit of white treesilk, stood quiet as a statue in the gray light; her voice was tranquil.

"One hundred and eleven years ago, the Government of Brasil-America sent several thousand people to this world. Fifty-six years ago, the Government of Canamerica sent two thousand more. The two groups have not merged, but have cooperated; and by now the City and the Town, though still distinct, are deeply interdependent.

"The first decades, for each group, were very hard; there were many deaths. There have been fewer, as we learned how to live here. The Registry has been discontinued for years, but we estimate the population of the City as about eight thousand, and the population of Shantih, at our last count, was four thousand three hundred and twenty."

There was a movement of surprise on the benches.

"Twelve thousand in the Songe Bay region is all the area can feed, we think, without over-intensive farming and a constant risk of famine. So we think it's time for some of us to move out and start a new settlement. There is, after all, a good deal of room."

Falco, up on his Councillor's chair, smiled faintly.

"Because the Town and City haven't merged, but still form two separate groups, we feel that a joint attempt to make a new settlement would be unwise. The pioneers will have to live together, work together, depend on one another, and, of course, intermarry. The strain of trying to keep up two social castes, in such a situation, would be intolerable. Anyhow, those who want to start a new settlement are all Shantih people.

"About two hundred and fifty families, some thousand people, are considering going north. They won't go all at once, but a couple of hundred at a time. As they go, their places on the farms will be filled by young people who stay here, and also, since the City is getting rather full, some City families may want to move out onto the land. They will be welcome. Even though a fifth of our farmers go north, there should be no drop in food production; and of course there'll be a thousand less mouths to feed.

"This is our plan. We trust that by discussion, criticism, and mutual striving toward truth, we may arrive together at full agreement on a matter which concerns us all."

There was a brief silence.

A man on one of the benches got up to speak, but sat down hastily when he saw Councillor Falco was about to speak.

"Thank you, Senhora Adelson," Falco said. "You will be informed of the Council's decision concerning this proposal. Senhor Brown, what is the next item on the agenda?"

The curly clerk made frantic gestures at the Shantih people with one hand while trying to find his place among the papers on his desk with the other. The two guards came forward briskly and flanked the five townspeople. "Come on!" one of them ordered.

"Excuse me," Vera said to them, gently. "Councillor Falco, I'm afraid we're misunderstanding one another again. We have made a decision, a tentative one. We wish now, in cooperation with you, to make a definite one. Neither we, nor you, can decide alone upon a matter which concerns us all."

"You misunderstand," Falco said, looking at the air above Vera's head. "You have made a proposal. The decision is up to the Government of Victoria."

Vera smiled. "I know you're not used to women speaking at your meetings, maybe it would go better if Jan Serov speaks for us." She stepped back, and a big, fair-skinned man replaced her. "You see," he said, as if continuing Vera's sentence, "first we have to settle what we want and how to do it, and then when we've agreed on that, we do it."

"The topic is closed," said bald Councillor Helder, at Falco's left on the dais. "If you continue to obstruct the business of the Plenum you must be forcibly removed."

"We aren't obstructing business, we're trying to get it done," Jan said. He didn't know what to do with his big hands, which hung uneasily at his sides, half-closed, wanting the handle of an absent hoe. "We have to talk this business over."

Falco said very quietly, "Guards."

As the guards pressed forward again, Jan looked in perplexity at Vera, and Hari spoke up: "Oh, now, calm down, Councillor, all we want is a bit of sensible talk, you can see that."

"Your Excellency! Have these people taken out!" shouted a man from the benches, and others started calling out, as if they wanted to be heard doing so by the Councillors on the dais. The Shantih people stood quiet, though Jan Serov and young King stared rather wide-eyed at the angry, shouting faces turned toward them. Falco conferred a moment with Helder, then signaled one of the guards, who left the hall at a run. Falco raised his hand for silence.

"You people," he said quite gently, "must understand that you aren't members of the Government, but subjects of the Government. To 'decide' upon some 'plan' contrary to the Government's decision is an act of rebellion. To make this clear to you, and the rest of your people, you'll be detained here until we are certain that normal order is restored."

"What's 'detained'?" Hari whispered to Vera, who said, "Prison." Hari nodded. He had been born in a prison, in Canamerica; he didn't remember it, but he was proud of it.

Eight guards now came shoving in and began to hustle the Shantih people to the door. "Single file! Hurry up now! Don't run or I'll shoot!" their officer commanded. None of the five showed the least sign of trying to run, resist, or protest. King, shoved by an impatient guard, said, "Oh, sorry," as if he had got in the way of someone in a rush.

The guards bundled the group out past the frescoes, under the columns, into the street. There they stopped. "Where to?" one asked the officer.

"Jail."

"Her too?"

They all looked at Vera, neat and delicate in her white silk. She looked back at them with tranquil interest.

"The boss said jail," the officer said, scowling.

"Hesumeria, sir, we can't stick her in there," said a little, sharp-eyed, scar-faced guard.

"That's what the boss said."

"But look, she's a lady."

"Take her to Boss Falco's house and let him decide when he gets home," suggested another, Scarface's twin, but scarless.

"I'll give you my word to stay wherever you decide, but I'd rather stay with my friends," said Vera.

"Please shut up, lady!" the officer said, clutching his head. "All right. You two take her to Casa Falco."

"The others will give their word too, if—" Vera began, but the officer turned his back on her and shouted, "All right! Get going! Single file!"

"This way, senhora," said Scarface.

At the turning Vera paused and held up her hand to salute her four companions, now far down the street. "Peace! Peace!" Hari shouted back, enthusiastically. Scarface muttered something and spat thickly aside. The two guards were men Vera would have been afraid of if she had passed them in a City street alone, but as they walked now, flanking her, their protectiveness of her was evident even in their gait. She realized that they felt themselves to be her rescuers.

"Is the jail very disagreeable?" she asked.

"Drunks, fights, stink," Scarface replied, and his twin added with grave propriety, "No place for a lady, senhora."

"Is it any better place for a man?" she inquired, but neither answered.

Casa Falco stood only three streets from the Capitol:

a big, low, white building with a red tile roof. The plump housemaid who came to the door was flustered by the presence of two soldiers and an unknown senhora on the doorstep; she curtseyed and panted and whispered, "Oh, hesumeria! Oh, hesumeria!" —and fled, leaving them on the doorstep. After a long pause, during which Vera conversed with her guards and found that they were indeed twin brothers, named Emiliano and Anibal, and that they liked their work as guards because they got good pay and didn't have to take any lip off anybody, but Anibal—Scarface— didn't like standing around so much because it made his feet hurt and his ankles swell—after this, a girl entered the front hall, a straight-backed, red-cheeked girl in sweeping full skirts. "I am Senhorita Falco," she said, with a quick glance at the guards, but speaking to Vera. Then her face changed. "Senhora Adelson, I didn't recognize you. I'm sorry. Please come in!"

"This is embarrassing, my dear, you see, I'm not a visitor, I'm a prisoner. These gentlemen have been very kind. They thought the jail had no place for women, so they brought me here. I think they have to come in too, if I come in, to guard me."

Luz Marina's eyebrows had come down in a fine, straight line. She stood silent for a moment. "They can wait in the entrance here," she said. "Sit on those chests," she said to Anibal and Emiliano. "Senhora Adelson will be with me."

The twins edged stiffly through the door after Vera.

"Please come in," Luz said, standing aside with formal courtesy, and Vera entered the hall of Casa

Falco, with its cushioned wooden chairs and settees, its inlaid tables and patterned stone floor, its thick glass windows and huge cold fireplaces, her prison. "Please sit down," said her jailer, and went to an inner door to order a fire laid and lighted, and coffee brought.

Vera did not sit down. As Luz returned toward her she looked at the girl with admiration. "My dear, you are kind and courteous. But I really am under arrest—by your father's order."

"This is my house," Luz said. Her voice was as dry as Falco's. "It is a house hospitable to guests."

Vera gave a docile little sigh, and sat down. Her gray hair had been blown about by the wind in the streets; she smoothed it back, then clasped her thin, brown hands in her lap.

"Why did he arrest you?" The question had been suppressed, and shot out under pressure. "What did you do?"

"Well, we came and tried to talk with the Council about plans for the new settlement."

"Did you know they'd arrest you?"

"We discussed it as one possibility."

"But what is it all about?"

"About the new settlement—about freedom, I suppose. But really, my dear, I mustn't talk about it with you. I've promised to be a prisoner, and prisoners aren't supposed to preach their crime."

"Why not?" said Luz disdainfully. "Is it catching, like a cold?"

Vera laughed. "Yes! —I know we've met, I don't know where it was."

The flustered maid hurried in with a tray, set it

on the table, and hurried out again, panting. Luz poured the black, hot drink—called coffee, made from the roasted root of a native plant—into cups of fine red earthenware.

"I was at the festival in Shanty Town a year ago," she said. The authoritative dryness was gone from her voice; she sounded shy. "To see the dancing. And there were a couple of times you spoke at school."

"Of course! You and Lev and all that lot were in school together! You knew Timmo, then. You know he died, on the journey north?"

"No. I didn't. In the wilderness," the girl said, and a brief silence followed the word. "Was Lev— Is Lev in jail now?"

"He didn't come with us. You know, in a war, you don't put all your soldiers in the same place at once." Vera, with recovered cheerfulness, sipped her coffee, and winced very slightly at the taste.

"A war?"

"Well, a war without fighting, of course. Maybe a rebellion, as your father says. Maybe, I hope, just a disagreement." Luz still looked blank. "You know what a war is?"

"Oh, yes. Hundreds of people killing each other. History of Earth at school was full of them. But I thought . . . your people wouldn't fight?"

"No," Vera agreed. "We don't fight. Not with knives and guns. But when we've agreed that something ought to be done, or not done, we get very stubborn. And when that meets up with another stubbornness, it can make a kind of war, a struggle of ideas, the only kind of war anybody ever wins. You see?"

Luz evidently did not.

"Well," Vera said comfortably, "you will see."

4

The ringtree of Victoria led a double life. It began as a single, fast-growing seedling with serrated red leaves. When it matured it flowered lavishly with large, honey-colored blossoms. Wotsits and other small flying creatures, attracted by the sweet-tasting petals, ate them, and while doing so fertilized the bitter-flavored heart of the flower with pollen caught on their fur, scales, wings, or vanes. The fertilized remnant of the flower curled itself up into a hard-shelled seed. There might be hundreds of these on the tree, but they dried up and dropped off, one after another, leaving at last one single seed on a high central branch. This seed, hard and ill-flavored, grew and grew while its tree weakened and withered, until the leafless branches drooped sadly beneath the big, heavy, black ball of the seed. Then, some afternoon when the autumn sun shone through gaps in the rainclouds, the seed performed its extraordinary feat: time-ripened and sun-warmed, it exploded. It went off with a bang that could be heard for miles. A cloud of dust and fragments rose and drifted slowly off across the hills. All was over, apparently, with the ringtree.

But in a circle around the central stem, several hundred seedlets, exploded from the shell, were burrowing themselves with energy down into the damp rich dirt. A year later the shoots were already competing for root-room; the less hardy ones died. Ten years later, and for a century or two after that, from twenty to sixty copper-leaved trees stood in a perfect ring about the long-vanished central stem. Branch and root, they stood apart, yet touching, forty ringtrees, one tree-ring. Once every eight or ten years they flowered and bore a small edible fruit, the seeds of which were excreted by wotsits, pouchbats, far-fallies, tree-coneys, and other fruit lovers. Dropped in the right spot, a seed germinated and produced the single tree; and it the single seed; and the cycle was repeated, from ringtree to tree-ring, timelessly.

Where the soil was favorable the rings grew inter-locking, but otherwise no large plants grew in the central circle of each ring, only grasses, moss, and ferns. Very old rings so exhausted their central ground that it might sink and form a hollow, which filled with ground seepage and with rain, and the circle of high, old dark-red trees was then mirrored in the still water of a central pool. The center of a tree-ring was always a quiet place. The ancient, pool-centered rings were the most quiet, the most strange.

The Meeting House of Shantih stood outside town in a vale which contained such a ring: forty-six trees rearing their columnar trunks and bronze crowns around a silent circle of water, rough with rain, or cloud-gray, or bright with sunlight flashing through red foliage from a sky briefly clear. Roots of the trees grew gnarled at the water's edge, making seats for the solitary contemplater. A single pair of herons lived in the Meeting-House Ring. The Victorian heron was not a heron; it was not even a bird. To describe their new world the exiles had had only words from their old world. The creatures that lived by the pools, one pair to a pool, were stilt-legged, pale-gray fish eaters: so they were herons. The first generation had known that they were not really herons, that they were not birds, nor reptiles, nor mammals. The following generations did not know what they were not, but did, in a way, know what they were. They were herons.

They seemed to live as long as the trees. Nobody had ever seen a baby heron, or an egg. Sometimes they danced, but if a mating followed the dance it was in the secrecy of the wilderness night, unseen. Silent, angular, elegant, they nested in the drifts of red leaves among the roots, and fished for water creatures in the shallows, and gazed across the pool at human beings with large, round eyes as colorless as water. They showed no fear of man, but never allowed a close approach.

The settlers of Victoria had never yet come upon any large land animal. The biggest herbivore was the coney, a fat slow rabbity beast with fine waterproof scales all over it; the biggest predator was the larva, red-eyed and shark-toothed, half a meter long. In captivity the larvas bit and screeched in insane frenzy till they died; the coneys refused to eat, lay down quietly, and died. There were big creatures in the sea; "whales" came into Songe Bay and were caught for food every summer; out at sea beasts huger than the whales had been seen, enormous, like writhing islands. The whales were not whales, but what the monsters were or were not, nobody knew. They never came near fishing boats. And the beasts of the plains and forests never came near, either. They did not run away. They simply kept their distance. They watched for a while, with clear eyes, and then moved away, ignoring the stranger.

Only the bright-winged farfallies and the wotsits ever consented to come near. Caged, a farfallie folded its wings and died; but if you put out honey for it, it might set up housekeeping on your roof, constructing there the little nest-like rain-cup in which, being semiaquatic, it slept. Wotsits evidently trusted in their peculiar ability to look like something else every few minutes. Occasionally they showed a positive desire to fly round and round a human being, or even to sit on him. Their shape-changing had in it an element of eye-fooling, perhaps of hypnosis, and Lev had sometimes wondered if the wotsits liked to use human beings to practice their tricks on. In any case, if you caged a wotsit, it turned into a shapeless brown lump like a clod of dirt, and after two or three hours, died.

None of the creatures of Victoria would be tamed, would live with man. None of them would approach him. They evaded; they slipped away, into the rain-shadowed, sweet-scented forests, or into the deep sea, or into death. They had nothing to do with man. He was a stranger. He did not belong.

"I had a cat," Lev's grandmother used to tell him, long ago. "A fat, gray cat with fur like the softest, softest treesilk. He had black stripes on his legs, and green eyes. He'd jump up on my lap, and put his nose under my ear, so I could hear him, and purr, and purr—like this!" The old lady would make a deep, soft, rumbling noise, to which the little boy listened with intense delight.

"What did he say when he was hungry, Nana?" He held his breath.

"PRRREEOWW! PRRREEOWW!"

She laughed, and he laughed.

There was only one another. The voices, the faces, the hands, the holding arms, of one's own kind. The other people, the other aliens.

Outside the doors, beyond the small plowed fields, lay the wilderness, the endless world of hills and red leaves and mist, where no voice spoke. To speak, there, no matter what you said, was to say, "I am a stranger."

"Some day," the child said, "I'll go and explore the whole world."

It was a new idea he had had, and he was full of it. He was going to make maps, and everything. But Nana wasn't listening. She had the sad look. He knew what to do about that. He came up quietly next to her and nuzzled in her neck below the ear, saying, "Prrrrr...."

"Is that my cat Mino? Hello, Mino! Why," she said, "it isn't Mino, it's Levuchka! What a surprise!"

He sat on her lap. Her large, old, brown arms were around him. On each wrist she wore a bangle of fine red soapstone. Her son Alexander, Sasha, Lev's father, had carved them for her. "Manacles," he had said when he gave them to her on her birthday. "Victoria manacles, Mama." And all the grown-ups had laughed, but Nana had had the sad look while she laughed.

"Nana. Was Mino Mino's name?"

"Of course, silly."

"But why?"

"Because I named him Mino."

"But animals don't have names."

"No. Not here."

"Why don't they?"

"Because we don't know their names," the grand-mother said, looking out over the small plowed fields.

"Nana."

"Well?" said the soft voice in the soft bosom against which his ear was pressed.

"Why didn't you bring Mino here?"

"We couldn't bring anything on the space ship. Nothing of our own. There wasn't room. But any-how, Mino was dead long before we came. I was a child when he was a kitten, and I was still a child when he was old and died. Cats don't live long, just a few years."

"But people live a long time."

"Oh, yes. A very long time."

Lev sat still on her lap, pretending he was a cat, with gray fur like the down of the cottonwool, only warm. "Prrr," he said softly, while the old woman sitting on the doorstep held him and gazed over his head at the land of her exile.

As he sat now on the hard broad root of a ringtree at the edge of the Meeting Pool, he thought of Nana, of the cat, of the silver water of Lake Serene, of the mountains above it which he longed to climb, of climbing the mountains out of the mist and rain into the ice and brightness of the summits; he thought of many things, too many things. He sat still, but his

mind would not be still. He had come here for stillness, but his mind raced, raced from past to future
and back again. Only for a moment did he find quiet.
One of the herons walked silently out into the water
from the far side of the pool. Lifting its narrow head
it gazed at Lev. He gazed back, and for an instant
was caught in that round transparent eye, as depthless
as the sky clear of clouds; and the moment was round,
transparent, silent, a moment at the center of all
moments, the eternal present moment of the silent
animal.

The heron turned away, bent its head, searching
the dark water for fish.

Lev stood up, trying to move as quietly and deftly
as the heron itself, and left the circle of the trees,
passing between two of the massive red trunks. It was
like going through a door into a different place entirely. The shallow valley was bright with sunlight,
the sky windy and alive; sun gilt the red-painted
timber roof of the Meeting House, which stood on the
south-facing slope. A good many people were at the
Meeting House already, standing on the steps and
porch talking, and Lev quickened his pace. He
wanted to run, to shout. This was no time for stillness. This was the first morning of the battle, the
beginning of victory.

Andre hailed him: "Come on! Everybody's waiting
for Boss Lev!"

He laughed, and ran; he came up the six steps of
the porch in two strides. "All right, all right, all right,"
he said, "what kind of discipline is this, where are
your boots, do you consider that a respectful position,

Sam?" Sam, a brown, stocky man wearing only white trousers, was standing calmly on his head near the porch railing.

Elia took charge of the meeting. They did not go inside, but sat around on the porch to talk, for the sunlight was very pleasant. Elia was in a serious mood, as usual, but Lev's arrival had cheered the others up, and the discussion was lively but brief. The sense of the meeting was clear almost at once. Elia wanted another delegation to go to the City to talk with the Bosses, but no one else did; they wanted a general meeting of the people of Shantih. They arranged that it would take place before sundown, and the younger people undertook to notify outlying villages and farms. As Lev was about to leave, Sam, who had serenely stood on his head throughout the discussion, came upright in a single graceful motion and said to Lev, smiling, "Arjuna, it will be a great battle."

Lev, his mind busy with a hundred things, smiled at Sam and strode off.

The campaign which the people of Shantih were undertaking was a new thing to them, and yet a familiar one. All of them, in the Town school and the Meeting House, had learned its principles and tactics; they knew the lives of the hero-philosophers Gandhi and King, and the history of the People of the Peace, and the ideas that had inspired those lives, that history. In exile, the People of the Peace had continued to live by those ideas; and so far had done so with success. They had at least kept themselves independent, while taking over the whole farming enterprise of the community, and sharing the produce fully and freely with the City. In exchange, the City provided them tools and machinery made by the Government ironworks, fish caught by the City fleet, and various other products which the older-established colony could more easily provide. It had been an arrangement satisfactory to both.

But gradually the terms of the bargain had grown more unequal. Shantih raised the cottonwool plants and the silktrees, and took the raw stuff to the City mills to be spun and woven. But the mills were very slow; if the townsfolk needed clothes, they did better to spin and weave the cloth themselves. The fresh and dried fish they expected did not arrive. Bad catches, the Council explained. Tools were not replaced. The City had furnished the farmers tools; if the farmers were careless with them it was up to them to replace them, said the Council. So it went on, gradually enough that no crisis arose. The people of Shantih compromised, adjusted, made do. The children and grandchildren of the exiles, now grown men and women, had never seen the technique of conflict and resistance, which was the binding force of their community, in action.

But they had been taught it: the spirit, the reasons, and the rules. They had learned it, and practiced it in the minor conflicts that arose within the Town itself. They had watched their elders arrive, sometimes by passionate debate and sometimes by almost wordless consent, at solutions to problems and disagreements. They had learned how to listen for the sense of the meeting, not the voice of the loudest. They had learned that they must judge each time whether obedience was necessary and right, or misplaced and wrong. They had learned that the act of violence is the act of weakness, and that the spirit's strength lies in holding fast to the truth.

At least they believed all that, and believed that they had learned it beyond any shadow of a doubt. Not one of them, under any provocation, would resort to violence. They were certain, and they were strong.

"It won't be easy, this time," Vera had said to them, before she and the others left for the City. "You know, it won't be easy."

They nodded, smiling, and cheered her. Of course it wouldn't be easy. Easy victories aren't worth winning.

As he went from farm to farm southwest of Shantih, Lev asked people to come to the big meeting, and answered their questions about Vera and the other hostages. Some of them were afraid of what the City men might do next, and Lev said, "Yes, they may do worse than take a few hostages. We can't expect them simply to agree with us, when we don't agree with them. We're in for a fight."

"But when they fight they use knives—and there's that—that whipping place, you know," said a woman, lowering her voice. "Where they punish their thieves and. . . ." She did not finish. Everyone else looked ashamed and uneasy.

"They're caught in the circle of violence that brought them here," said Lev. "We aren't. If we stand firm, all of us together, then they'll see our strength; they'll see it's greater than theirs. They'll begin to listen to us. And to win free, themselves." His face and voice were so cheerful as he spoke that the farmers could see that he was speaking the simple truth, and began to look forward to the next confrontation with the City instead of dreading it. Two brothers with names taken from the Long March, Lyons and Pamplona, got especially worked up; Pamplona, who was rather simple, followed Lev around from farm to farm the rest of the morning so he could hear the Resistance Plans ten times over.

In the afternoon Lev worked with his father and the other three families that farmed their bog-rice paddy, for the last harvest was ripe and must be got in no matter what else was going on. His father went on with one of these families for supper; Lev went to eat with Southwind. She had left her mother's house and was living alone in the little house west of town which she and Timmo had built when they married. It stood by itself in the fields, though within sight of the nearest group of houses outlying from the town. Lev, or Andre, or Martin's wife Italia, or all three of them, often came there for supper, bringing something to share with Southwind. She and Lev ate together, sitting on the doorstep, for it was a mild, golden autumn afternoon, and then went on together to the Meeting House, where two or three hundred people were already gathered, and more coming every minute.

Everyone knew what they were there for: to reassure one another that they were all together, and to discuss what was to be done next. The spirit of the gathering was festive and a little excited. People stood up on the porch and spoke, all saying in one way

or another, "We're not going to give in, we're not
going to let our hostages down!" When Lev spoke he
was cheered: grandson of the great Shults who led the
Long March, explorer of the wilderness, and a general
favorite anyhow. The cheering was interrupted, there
was a commotion in the crowd, which now numbered
over a thousand. Night had come on, and the electric
lights on the Meeting House porch, powered by the
town generator, were feeble, so it was hard to see
what was going on at the edge of the crowd. A squat,
massive, black object seemed to be pushing through
the people. When it got nearer the porch it could be
seen as a mass of men, a troop of guards from the City,
moving as a solid block. The block had a voice: "Meetings . . . order . . . pain," was all anyone could hear,
because everyone was asking indignant questions.
Lev, standing under the light, called for quiet, and
as the crowd fell silent the loud voice could be heard:

"Mass meetings are forbidden, the crowd is to disperse. Public meetings are forbidden by order of the
Supreme Council upon pain of imprisonment and
punishment. Disperse at once and go to your homes!"

"No," people said, "why should we?"—"What right
have they got?"—"Go to your own homes!"

"Come on, quiet!" Andre roared, in a voice nobody
knew he possessed. As they grew quiet again he said to
Lev in his usual mumble, "Go on, talk."

"This delegation from the City has a right to speak,"
Lev said, loud and clear. "And to be heard. And
when we've heard what they say, we may disregard it,
but remember that we are resolved not to threaten by

act or word. We do not offer anger or injury to these men who come amongst us. What we offer them is friendship and the love of truth!"

He looked at the guards, and the officer at once repeated the order to disperse the meeting in a flat, hurried voice. When he was through, there was silence. The silence continued. Nobody said anything. Nobody moved.

"All right now," the officer shouted, forcing his voice, "get moving, disperse, go to your homes!"

Lev and Andre looked at each other, folded their arms, and sat down. Holdfast, who was also up on the porch, sat down too; then Southwind, Elia, Sam, Jewel, and the others. The people on the meeting ground began to sit down. It was a queer sight in the shadows and the yellowish, shadow-streaked light: the many, many dark forms all seeming to shrink to half their height, with a faint rustling sound, a few murmurs. Some children giggled. Within half a minute they were all sitting down. No one remained afoot but the troop of guards, twenty men standing close together.

"You've been warned," the officer shouted, and his voice was both vindictive and embarrassed. He was evidently not sure what to do with these people who now sat silently on the ground, looking at him with expressions of peaceable curiosity, as if they were children at a puppet show and he was the puppet. "Get up and disperse, or I'll begin the arrests!"

Nobody said anything.

"All right, arrest the thir—the twenty nearest. Get up. You, get up!"

The people spoken to or laid hands on by the guardsmen got up, and stood quietly. "Can my wife come too?" a man asked the guard in a low voice, not wanting to break the great, deep stillness of the crowd.

"There will be no further mass meetings of any kind. By order of the Council!" the officer bawled, and led his troop off, herding a group of about twenty-five townsfolk. They disappeared into the darkness outside the reach of the electric lights.

Behind them the crowd was silent.

A voice rose from it, singing. Other voices joined in, softly at first. It was an old song, from the days of the Long March on Earth.

> O when we come,
> O when we come to the Free Land
> Then we will build the City,
> O when we come. . . .

As the group of guards and prisoners went on into the darkness the singing did not sound fainter behind them but stronger and clearer, as all the hundreds of voices joined and sent the music ringing over the dark quiet lands between Shantih and the City of Victoria.

The twenty-four people who had been arrested by the guards, or had voluntarily gone off with them, returned to Shantih late the following day. They had been put into a warehouse for the night, perhaps because the City Jail had no room for so many, and sixteen of them women and children. There had been a trial in the afternoon, they said, and when it was done they were told to go home. "But we're supposed to pay a fine," old Pamplona said importantly.

Pamplona's brother Lyons was a thriving orcharder, but Pamplona, slow and sickly, had never amounted to much. This was his moment of glory. He had gone to prison, just like Gandhi, just like Shults, just like on Earth. He was a hero, and delighted.

"A fine?" Andre asked, incredulous. "Money? They know we don't use their coins—"

"A fine," Pamplona explained, tolerant of Andre's ignorance, "is that we have to work for twenty days on the new farm."

"What new farm?"

"Some kind of new farm the Bosses are going to make."

"The Bosses are going in for farming?" Everybody laughed.

"They'd better, if they want to eat," a woman said.

"What if you don't go work on this new farm?"

"I don't know," Pamplona said, getting confused. "Nobody said. We weren't supposed to talk. It was a court, with a judge. The judge talked."

"Who was the judge?"

"Macmilan."

"Young Macmilan?"

"No, the old one, the Councillor. The young one was there, though. A big fellow he is! Like a tree! And he smiles all the time. A fine young man."

Lev came, at a run, having just got news of the prisoners' return. He hugged the first ones he came to, in the excited group that had gathered in the street to welcome them. "You're back, you're back— All of you?"

"Yes, yes, they're all back, you can go eat supper now!"

"The others, Hari and Vera—"

"No, not them. They didn't see them."

"But all of you— They didn't hurt you?"

"Lev said he couldn't eat anything till you got back, he's been fasting."

"We're all right, go eat some dinner, what a stupid thing to do!"

"They treated you well?"

"Like guests, like guests," old Pamplona asserted. "We're all brothers. Isn't that so? A good big breakfast they gave us, too!"

"Our own rice we grew, that's what they gave us. Fine hosts! to lock their guests up in a barn as black as night and as cold as last night's porridge, I have an ache in every bone and I want a bath, every one of those guard people was crawling with lice, I saw one right on his neck, the one that arrested me, a louse the size of your fingernail, ugh, I want a bath!" This was Kira, a buxom woman who lisped because she had lost her two front teeth; she said she didn't miss the teeth, they got in the way of her talking anyhow. "Who'll put me up for the night? I'm not going to walk home to East Village with every bone aching and a dozen lice creeping up and down my backbone!" Five or six people at once offered her a bath, a bed, hot food. All the freed prisoners were looked after and made much of. Lev and Andre went off down the little side street that led to Lev's home. They walked in silence for a while.

"Thank God!" said Lev.

"Yes. Thank God. They're back; it worked. If only Vera and Jan and the others had come back with them."

"They're all right. But this lot——none of them was ready, they hadn't thought about it, they hadn't prepared themselves. I was afraid they'd be hurt, I was afraid they'd be frightened, get angry. It was our responsibility, we led the sit-down. We got them arrested. But they held out. They weren't frightened, they didn't fight, they held fast!" Lev's voice shook. "It was my responsibility."

"Ours," Andre said. "We didn't send them, you didn't send them; they went. They chose to go. You're worn out, you ought to eat. Sasha!" They were at the door of the house. "Make this man eat. They fed his prisoners, now you feed him."

Sasha, sitting by the hearth sanding down a hoe handle, looked up; his mustache bristled, his eyebrows bristled over his deep-set eyes. "Who can make my son do what he doesn't want to do?" he said. "If he wants to eat, he knows where the soup bowl is."

5

The Senhor Councillor Falco gave a dinner party. During most of it, he wished sincerely that he had not given a dinner party.

It was to be a party in the old style, the Old World style, with five courses, and fine clothes, and conversation, and music after dinner. The old men arrived at the hour, each accompanied by his wife and an unmarried daughter or two. Some of the younger men, such as young Helder, also arrived on time, with their wives. The women stood about the fireplace at one end of the hall of Casa Falco in their long gowns and jewelry, and chattered; the men stood about the fireplace at the other end of the hall in their best black suits, and talked. All seemed to be going well, just as it had gone when Councillor Falco's grandfather Don Ramon had given dinner parties, just like dinner parties back on Earth, as Don Ramon had often said with satisfaction and conviction, for after all his father Don Luis had been born on Earth and had been the greatest man in Rio de Janeiro.

But some of the guests had not come on time. It got later, and still they did not come. Councillor Falco was summoned by his daughter to the kitchen: the cooks' faces were tragic, the superb dinner would be ruined. At his command the long table was carried into the hall and set, the guests sat down, the first course was served, eaten, cleared away, the second course was served, and then, only then, in came young Macmilan, young Marquez, young Weiler, free and easy, without an apology and, what was worse, with a whole rabble of their friends, uninvited: seven or eight big bucks with whips in their belts and broad-brimmed hats which they didn't know enough to take off indoors, and dirty boots, and a lot of loud dirty talk. New places had to be set, crowded in

among the others. The young men had been drinking
before they came, and went on swilling Falco's best
ale. They pinched the maidservants, but ignored the
ladies. They shouted across the table, and blew
their noses in the embroidered napkins. When the
supreme moment of the dinner arrived, the meat
course, roast coney—Falco had hired ten trappers
for a week to supply this luxury—the latecomers piled
their plates so greedily that there was not enough to
go round, and no one at the foot of the table got
meat. The same thing happened with the dessert, a
molded pudding made with root starch, boiled fruits,
and nectar. Several of the young men scooped it
out of the bowls with their fingers.

Falco signaled his daughter, at the foot of the table,
and she led a retreat of the ladies to the garden sitting
room at the back of the house. This left the young
toughs all the more freedom to lounge, spit, belch,
swear, and get drunker. Small cups of the brandy
for which the stillrooms of Casa Falco were famous
got tossed off like water, and the young men yelled
at the bewildered servants to refill. Some of the other
young men, and some of the older ones, liked this
crude behavior, or perhaps thought it was how one
was expected to behave at a dinner party, and joined
in it. Old Helder got so drunk he went and vomited
in the corner, but he came back to table and started
drinking again.

Falco and some close friends, the elder Marquez,
Burnier, and the doctor, withdrew to the hearth and
tried to talk; but the noise around the long table was
deafening. Some were dancing, some quarreling; the

musicians hired to play after dinner had mixed in with the guests and were drinking like fish; young Marquez had a serving girl on his lap, where she sat white-faced and cringing, muttering, "Oh hesumeria! Oh hesumeria!"

"A very merry party, Luis," old Burnier said, after a particularly painful outburst of song and screeching.

Falco had remained calm throughout; his face was calm as he replied, "A proof of our degeneration."

"The young fellows aren't used to such feasts. Only Casa Falco knows how to give a party in the old style, the real Earth style."

"They are degenerates," Falco said.

His brother-in-law Cooper, a man of sixty, nodded. "We have lost the style of Earth."

"Not at all," said a man behind them. They all turned. It was Herman Macmilan, one of the late-comers; he had been guzzling and shouting with the rest, but showed no signs of drunkenness now, except perhaps the heightened color of his handsome young face. "It seems to me, gentlemen, that we're rediscovering the style of Earth. After all, who were our ancestors that came from the Old World? Not weak, meek men, were they? Brave men, bold, strong men, who knew how to live. Now we're learning again how to live. Plans, laws, rules, manners, what's that got to do with us? Are we slaves, women? What are we afraid of? We're men, free men, masters of a whole world. It's time we came into our inheritance; that's how it is, gentlemen." He smiled, deferential, yet perfectly self-confident.

Falco was impressed. Perhaps this wreck of a dinner

party might serve some purpose after all. This young Macmilan, who had never seemed anything but a fine muscular animal, a likely future match for Luz Marina, was showing both willpower and brains, the makings of a man. "I agree with you, Don Herman," he said. "But I'm able to agree with you only because you and I are still able to talk. Unlike most of our friends there. A man must be able to drink and think. Since only you of the young men seem able to do both, tell me: what do you think of my idea of making latifundia?"

"Big farms, that means?"

"Yes. Big farms; large fields, planted in one crop, for efficiency. My idea is to pick managers from among our best young men; to give each a large region to run, an estate, and enough peasants to work it; and let him run it as he wishes. Thus more food will be produced. The excess population in Shanty Town will be put to work, and kept under control, to prevent any more talk about independence and new colonies. And the next generation of City Men will include a number of great estate owners. We've kept close together for strength long enough. It's time, as you said, that we spread out, use our freedom, make ourselves masters of this rich world of ours."

Herman Macmilan listened, smiling. His finely cut lips had an almost constant smile.

"Not a bad idea," he said. "Not a bad idea at all, Senhor Councillor."

Falco bore with his patronizing tone, because he had decided that Herman Macmilan was a man he could make use of.

"Consider it," he said. "Consider it for yourself." He knew young Macmilan was doing just that. "How would you like to own such an estate, Don Herman? A little—what's the word, an old word—"

"Kingdom," old Burnier supplied.

"Yes. A little kingdom for yourself. How does it strike you?" He spoke flatteringly, and Herman Macmilan preened himself. In the self-important, Falco reflected, there is always room for a little more self-importance.

"Not bad," Macmilan said, nodding judiciously.

"To carry out the plan, we'll need the vigor of you young men, and the brains. Opening up new farmland has always been a slow business. Forced labor is the only way to clear large areas quickly. If this unrest in Shanty Town goes on, we can have plenty of peasant rebels to sentence to forced labor. But, since they're all words and no actions, they may have to be pushed, we may have to crack the whip to make them fight, we may have to drive them to rebellion, you understand? How does that kind of action strike you?"

"A pleasure, senhor. Life's boring here. Action is what we want."

Action, Falco thought, is also what I want. I should like to knock this condescending young man's teeth out. But he is going to be useful, and I shall use him, and smile.

"That's what I hoped to hear! Listen, Don Herman. You have influence among the young men—a natural gift of leadership. Now tell me what you think of this. Our regular guards are loyal enough, but they're commoners, stupid men, easily confused by the Shanty-

Towners' tricks. What we need to lead them is a troop of elite soldiers, young aristocrats, brave, intelligent, and properly commanded. Men who love fighting, like our brave ancestors of Earth. Do you think such a troop could be brought together and trained? How would you suggest we go about it?"

"All you need is a leader," Herman Macmilan said without hesitation. "I could train up a group like that in a week or two."

After that night, young Macmilan became a frequent visitor at Casa Falco, coming in at least once a day to talk with the Councillor. Whenever Luz was in the front part of the house it seemed Macmilan was there; and she took to spending more and more time in her own room, or the attic, or the garden sitting room. She had always avoided Herman Macmilan, not because she disliked him, it was impossible to dislike anyone so handsome, but because it was humiliating to know that everybody, seeing Luz and Herman say a word to each other, was thinking and saying, "Ah, they'll be married soon." Whether he wanted to or not he brought the idea of marriage with him, constraining her too to think about it; and not wanting to think about it, she had always been very shy with him. Nowadays it was the same, except that, seeing him daily as a familiar of the house, she had decided that—although it was wasteful and a pity—you could dislike even a very handsome man.

He came into the back sitting room without knocking at the door, and stood in the doorway, a graceful and powerful figure in his tightly belted tunic. He surveyed the room, which faced inward on the large central garden around which the back part of the house was built. The garden doors stood open and the sound of fine mild rain falling on the paths and shrubs of the garden filled the room with quietness. "So this is where you hide away," he said.

Luz had risen when he appeared. She wore a dark homespun skirt and a white shirt that glimmered in the dim light. Behind her in the shadows another woman sat spinning with a drop spindle.

"Always hiding away here, eh?" Herman repeated. He came no farther into the room, perhaps waiting to be invited in, perhaps also conscious of his dramatic presence framed in the doorway.

"Good afternoon, Don Herman. Are you looking for my father?"

"I've just been talking to him."

Luz nodded. Though she was curious to know what Herman and her father talked about so much lately, she certainly wasn't going to ask. The young man came on into the room and stood in front of Luz, looking at her with his good-humored smile. He reached out and took her hand, raised it to his lips, and kissed it. Luz pulled away in a spasm of annoyance. "That is a stupid custom," she said, turning away.

"All customs are stupid. But the old folks can't get on without them, eh? They think the world would fall apart. Hand-kissing, bowing, senhor this and senhora that, how it was done on the Old World, history, books, rubbish. . . . Well!"

Luz laughed in spite of herself. It was fine to hear

Herman simply brush away as nonsense the things that loomed so large and worrisome in her life.

"The Black Guards are coming on very well," he said. "You must come see us train. Come tomorrow morning."

"What 'Black Guards'?" she asked disdainfully, sitting down and taking up her work, a bit of fine sewing for Eva's expected fourth child. That was the trouble with Herman, if you once smiled or said something natural or felt like admiring him, he pushed in, pushed his advantage, and you had to snub him at once.

"My little army," he replied. "What's that?" He sat down beside her on the wicker settee. There was not enough room for his big body and her slight one. She tugged her skirt out from under his thigh. "A bonnet," she said, trying to control her temper, which was rising. "For Evita's baby."

"Oh, God, yes, what a breeder that girl is! Aldo has his quiver full. We don't take married men in the Guards. A fine bunch they are. You have to come see them."

Luz made a microscopic embroidery knot, and no reply.

"I've been out looking over my land. That's why I wasn't here yesterday."

"I didn't notice," said Luz.

"Choosing my property. A valley down on Mill River. Fine country that is, once it's cleared. My house will be built up on a hill. I saw the site for it at once. A big house, like this one, but bigger, two stories, with porches all round. And barns and a smithy and so on.

Then, down in the valley near the river, the peasants'
huts, where I can look down on them. Bog-rice in the
marshes where the river spreads out in the valley
bottom. Orchards on the hillsides—treesilk and fruit.
I'll lumber some of the forests and save some for coney
hunting. A beautiful place it'll be, a kingdom. Come
and see it with me next time I go down there. I'll
send the pedicab from Casa Macmilan. It's too far
for a girl to walk. You should see it."

"What for?"

"You'll like it," Herman said with absolute con-
fidence. "How would you like to have a place like that
yourself? Own everything in sight. A big house, lots
of servants. Your own kingdom."

"Women aren't kings," Luz said. She bent her head
over a stitch. The light was really too dim now for
sewing, but it gave her the excuse not to look at
Herman. He kept looking at her, staring, his face
intent and expressionless; his eyes seemed darker
than usual and he had stopped smiling. But all at once
his mouth opened and he laughed, "Ha, ha!"—a
small laugh for so big a man. "No. All the same,
women have a way of getting what they want, don't
they, my little Luz?"

She sewed on and did not answer.

Herman put his face close to hers and whispered,
"Get rid of the old woman."

"What did you say?" Luz inquired in a normal
speaking voice.

"Get rid of her," Herman repeated, with a slight
nod.

Luz stuck her needle carefully into its case, folded

her sewing, and stood up. "Excuse me, Don Herman. I must go speak to the cook," she said, and went out. The other woman sat still, spinning. Herman sat for a minute sucking his lips; he smiled, got up, and sauntered out, his thumbs in his belt.

After a quarter-hour Luz looked in the doorway by which she had left, and seeing no Herman Macmilan, came back in. "That clod," she said, and spat on the floor.

"He's very good-looking," said Vera, teasing out a last shred of treesilk, twirling it into a fine even thread, and bringing the full spindle back to her lap.

"Very," said Luz. She picked up the neatly folded baby bonnet on which she had been working, looked at it, squashed it into a ball and threw it across the room. "Screw!" she said.

"The way he talked to you makes you angry," Vera said, half questioningly.

"The way he talks, the way he looks, the way he sits, the way he is. . . . Ugh! My little army, my big house, my servants, my peasants, my little Luz. If I were a man I'd knock his head on the wall till his big teeth fell out."

Vera laughed. She did not laugh often, usually only when she was startled. "No, you wouldn't!"

"I would. I'd kill him."

"Oh, no. No. You wouldn't. Because if you were a man, you'd know you were as strong as he, or stronger, and so you wouldn't have to prove it. The trouble is, being a woman, here, where they always tell you you're weak, you believe them. That was funny, when he said the South Valleys are too far for a girl to walk! About twelve kilometers!"

"I've never walked that far. Probably not half that far."

"Well, that's what I mean. They tell you you're weak and helpless. And if you believe it, you get mad and want to hurt people."

"Yes, I do," Luz said, facing around to Vera. "I want to hurt people. I want to and I probably will."

Vera sat still, looking up at the girl. "Yes." She spoke more gravely. "If you marry a man like that and live his life, then I agree. You may not really want to hurt people, but you will."

Luz stared back at her. "That is hateful," she said at last. "Hateful! To say it that way. That I haven't any choice, that I have to hurt people, that it doesn't even matter what I want."

"Of course it matters, what you want."

"It doesn't. That's the whole point."

"It does. And that's the whole point. *You* choose. You choose whether or not to make choices."

Luz stood there a minute longer, still staring at her. Her cheeks were still burning red with temper, but her eyebrows were not drawn down level; they were raised as if in surprise or fright, as if something altogether unexpected had risen up before her.

She moved indecisively, then went out the open door into the garden that lay at the heart of the house.

The touch of the sparse rain on her face was gentle.

Raindrops falling into the little fountain basin in the center of the garden made delicate interlocking rings, each ring gone in an instant of urgent outward motion, a ceaseless tremor of clear fleeting circles on the surface of the water in the round basin of gray stone.

House walls and shuttered windows stood all round the garden, silent. The garden was like an inner room of the house, shut in, protected. But a room with the roof taken off. A room into which rain fell.

Luz's arms were wet and cold. She shuddered. She returned to the door, the dim room where Vera sat.

She stood between Vera and the light and said in a rough, low voice, "What kind of man is my father?"

There was a pause. "Is it fair of you to ask me that? Or of me to answer? . . . Well, I suppose so. So what can I say? He's strong. He's a king, a real one."

"It's just a word, I don't know what it means."

"We have old stories—the king's son who rode on the tiger. . . . Well, I mean he's strong of soul, he has grandeur of heart. But when a man is shut up inside walls that he's been building stronger and higher all his life, then maybe no strength is enough. He can't get out."

Luz crossed the room, stooped to pick up the baby bonnet she had flung under a chair, and stood with her face turned from Vera, smoothing out the little scrap of half-embroidered cloth.

"Neither can I," she said.

"Oh, no, no," the older woman said energetically. "You're not inside the walls with him! He doesn't protect you—you protect him. When the wind blows, it doesn't blow on him, but on the roof and walls of this City that his fathers built as a fortress against the unknown, a protection. And you're part of that City, part of his roofs and walls, his house, Casa Falco. So is his title, Senhor, Councillor, Boss. So are all his servants and his guards, all the men and women he can give orders to. They're all part of his house, the walls to keep the wind off him. Do you see what I mean? I say it so foolishly. I don't know how to say it. What I mean is, I think your father is a man who should be a great man, but he's made a bad mistake. He has never come outside into the rain."

Vera began to wind the thread she had spun off the spindle into a skein, peering at it in the dim light. "And so, because he won't let himself be hurt, he does wrong to those he loves best. And then he sees that, and after all, it hurts him."

"Hurts *him*?" the girl said fiercely.

"Oh, that's the last thing we learn about our parents. The last thing, because after we learn it, they aren't our parents any longer, but just other people like us. . . ."

Luz sat down on the wicker settee and put the baby bonnet on her knee, continuing to smoothe it out carefully with two fingers. After quite a while she said, "I'm glad you came here, Vera."

Vera smiled and went on winding off the thread.

"I'll help with that."

On her knees, feeding the thread off the spindle so that Vera could wind it in even loops, she said, "It was stupid of me to say that. You want to go back to your family, you're in jail here."

"A very pleasant jail! And I have no family. Of course I want to go back. To come and go as I like."

"You never married?"

"There was so much else to do," Vera said, smiling and placid.

"So much else to do! There's nothing else to do, for us."

"No?"

"If you don't marry, you're an old maid. You make bonnets for other women's babies. You order the cook to make fish soup. You get laughed at."

"Are you afraid of that, being laughed at?"

"Yes. Very much." Luz spent some while untangling a length of thread that had snagged on the shank of the spindle. "I don't care if stupid people laugh," she said more quietly. "But I don't like to be scorned. And the scorn would be deserved. Because it takes courage to really be a woman, just as much as to be a man. It takes courage to really be married, and to bear children, and to bring them up."

Vera watched her face. "Yes. It does. Great courage. But, again, is that your only choice—marriage and motherhood, or nothing?"

"What else is there, for a woman? What else that really counts?"

Vera turned a little to look out the open doors into the gray garden. She sighed, a deep involuntary drawing of breath.

"I wanted a child very much," she said. "But you see, there were other things . . . that counted." She smiled faintly. "Oh, yes, it's a choice. But not the only one. One can be a mother and a great deal else besides. One can do more than one thing. With the will, and the luck. . . . My luck wasn't good, or maybe I was wrongheaded, made the wrong choice. I don't like compromise, you see. I set my heart on a man who . . . had his heart set on somebody else. That was Sasha—Alexander Shults, Lev's father. Oh, a long long time ago, before you were born. So he married, and I went on with the work I was good at, because it always interested me, but there weren't any other men who did. But even if I'd married did I have to sit in the back room all my life? You know, if we sit in the back room, with babies or without babies, and leave all the rest of the world to the men, then of course the men will do everything and be everything. Why should they? They're only half the human race. It's not fair to leave them all the work to do. Not fair to them or us. Besides," and she smiled more broadly, "I like men very much, but sometimes . . . they're so stupid, so stuffed with theories. . . . They go in straight lines only, and won't stop. It's dangerous to do that. It's dangerous to leave everything up to the men, you know. That's one reason why I'd like to go home, at least for a visit. To see what Elia with his theories, and my dear young Lev with his ideals, are up to. I get worried they'll go too fast and too straight and get us into a place we can't get out of, a trap. You see it seems to me that where men are weak and dangerous is in their vanity. A woman has a center, is a center. But a man isn't, he's a reaching out. So he reaches out and grabs things and piles them up around him and says, I'm this, I'm that, this is me, that's me, I'll prove that I am me! And he can wreck a lot of things, trying to prove it. That's what I was trying to say about your father. If he'd only be Luis Falco. That is quite enough. But no, he has to be the Boss, the Councillor, the Father, and so on. What a waste! And Lev, he's terribly vain too, maybe in the same way. A great heart, but not sure where the center is. Oh, I wish I could talk with him, just for ten minutes, and make sure. . . ." Vera had long since forgotten to wind her thread; she shook her head sadly and looked down at the skein with a faraway gaze.

"Go on, then," Luz said in a low voice.

Vera looked mildly puzzled.

"Go back to the Town. Tonight. I'll let you out. And I'll tell my father, tomorrow, that I did so. I can do something—something besides sit here and sew and swear and listen to that stupid Macmilan!"

Lithe, robust, and commanding, the girl had leapt to her feet and stood over Vera, who sat still, looking shrunken.

"I've given my word, Luz Marina."

"What does that matter?"

"If I don't speak truth I can't seek truth," Vera answered in a hard voice.

They stared at each other, their faces set.

"I have no child," Vera said, "and you have no mother. If I could help you, child, I would. But not that way. I keep my promises."

"I make no promises," Luz said.

She cleared a strand of thread from the spindle, Vera wound it onto the skein.

6

Whip butts rattled on doors. Men's voices rang out; down by River Farm somebody was shouting or screaming. Villagers huddled together in a group in the cold, smoke-scented fog; it was not daybreak yet, houses and faces were lost in the fog and dark. Inside the little houses children, frightened by their parents' fear and confusion, screamed aloud. People tried to get lamps lighted, to find their clothes, to hush the children. The City guards, excited, armed among the weaponless and clothed among the unclothed, flung open doors, shouldered into warm dark interiors of houses, shouted orders at the villagers and each other, pushed men one way and women another; their officer could have no control over them, dispersed as they were in the dark, among houses, and in the growing crowd in the one street of the village; only the docility of the villagers prevented the excitement of brutality from becoming the ecstasy of murder and rape. They protested, argued, and questioned verbally, but since most of them thought they were being arrested, and all had agreed at the Meeting House not to resist arrest, they obeyed the guards' orders as promptly as they could; when they understood the orders, they passed the information on readily and clearly—grown men out onto the street, women and children stay indoors—as the best means of self-protection; so the frantic officer found his prisoners rounding themselves up. As soon as there was a group of twenty or so, he told off four guards, one armed with a musket, to march them out of the village. Two such groups had been marched off from Tableland Village; the fourth from South Village was being brought together when Lev arrived. Lyons's wife Rosa had run from Tableland to Shantih, and, exhausted, had hammered at the Shultses' door, gasping, "They're taking off the men, the guards, they're taking off all the men." Lev had set off at once, alone, leaving Sasha to rouse the rest of the Town. As he came up, panting from the three-kilometer run, the fog was thinning, growing luminous; the figures of villagers and guards on the South Road bulked strangely in the half-light, as he cut across the fields to the head of the group. He stopped in front of the man at the head of the half-bunched, half-straggling line. "What's going on?"

"Labor draft. Get in line with the others."

Lev knew the guard, a tall fellow named Angel; they had been at school together for a year. Southwind and the other girls from Shantih had been afraid of Angel, because he cornered them in the hallway when he could and tried to handle them.

"Get in line," Angel repeated, and swung up his musket, resting the end of the barrel on Lev's chest. He was breathing almost as hard as Lev, and his eyes were widely dilated; he gave a kind of gasping laugh, watching how Lev's winded breathing made the gun barrel rise and fall. "You ever hear one of these go off, boy? Loud, loud, like a ringtree seed—" He pushed the musket harder against Lev's breastbone, then swung the gun up suddenly pointing at the sky, and fired.

Dazed by the terrific noise, Lev staggered back and stood staring. Angel's face had gone dead gray; he also stood blank for some seconds, shaken by the recoil of the crudely made gun.

The villagers behind Lev, thinking he had been shot, came surging forward, and the other guards ran with them, yelling and cursing; the long whips uncoiled and cracked, flickering weirdly in the fog. "I'm all right," Lev said. His voice sounded faint and distant inside his head. "I'm all right!" he shouted as loud as he could. He heard Angel also shouting, saw a villager take a whiplash straight across his face. "Get back in line!" He joined the group of villagers, and they huddled together, then, obeying the guards, strung out by twos and threes, and started to walk southward down the rough track.

"Why are we going south? This isn't the City Road, why are we going south?" the one next to him, a boy of eighteen or so, said in a ragged whisper.

"It's a labor draft," Lev said. "Some kind of work. How many have they taken?" He shook his head to rid it of a buzzing dizziness.

"All the men in our valley. Why do we have to go?"

"To bring the others back. When we're all together we can act together. It'll be all right. Nobody got hurt?"

"I don't know."

"It'll be all right. Hold fast," Lev whispered, not knowing what he was saying. He began to drop back through the others until he came alongside the man who had been whipped. He was walking with his arm across his eyes, another man was holding his shoulder to guide him; they were last in line; barely visible in the ground mist, a guard followed behind.

"Can you see?"

"I don't know," the man said, pressing his arm across his face. His gray hair stood up ruffled and tufted; he was wearing a nightshirt and trousers, and was barefoot; his broad bare feet looked curiously childlike, shuffling and stubbing on the rocks and mud of the road.

"Take your arm away, Pamplona," the other man said anxiously. "So we can have a look."

The guard following behind shouted something, a threat or an order to move along faster.

Pamplona lowered his arm. Both his eyes were shut; one was untouched, the other was lost in an open bleeding slash where the whipthong had cut from the corner of the brow to the bridge of the nose. "It hurts," he said. "What was it? I can't see, there's something in my eye. Lyons? Is that you? I want to go home."

More than a hundred men were taken from the villages and outlying farms south and west of Shantih to begin work on the new estates in South Valley. They got there in mid-morning, as the fog was lifting off Mill River in writhing banners. Several guards were posted out on the South Road to prevent trouble-makers from Shantih joining the forced-labor group. Tools were distributed, hoes, mattocks, brush-knives; and they were put to work in groups of four or five, each watched over by a guard armed with whip or musket. No barracks or shelters had been set up for them or for the thirty guards. When evening came, they built campfires of wet wood and slept on the wet ground. Food had been provided, but the bread had got rain-soaked so that most of it was a mass of dough. The guards grumbled bitterly among them-selves. The villagers talked, persistently. At first the officer in charge of the operation, Captain Eden, tried to forbid them from talking, fearing conspiracy; then, when he realized that one group among them was arguing with another lot who were for running off during the night, he let them talk. He had no way to prevent them from sneaking off by ones and twos in the darkness; guards were stationed about with muskets, but they couldn't see in the dark, there was no possibility of keeping bright fires going in the rain, and they had not been able to build a "com-pound area" as ordered. The villagers had worked hard at ground-clearing, but had proved inept and stupid at constructing any kind of fence or palisade out of the cut shrubs and brambles, and his own men would not lay down their weapons to do such work. Captain Eden set his men on watch and watch; he himself did not sleep that night.

In the morning the whole lot of them, his men and the villagers, still seemed to be there; everyone was slow-moving in the misty cold, and it took hours to get fires lighted and some kind of breakfast cooked and served out. Then the tools must be distributed again, the long hoes, the wicked steel brush-knives, mattocks, machetes. A hundred and twenty men armed with those, against thirty with whips and muskets. Didn't they see what they could so easily do? Under Captain Eden's disbelieving gaze the villagers filed past the heap of tools, just as they had done yesterday, took what they needed, and set to work again clearing the brush and undergrowth off the slope down to the river. They worked hard and well; they knew this kind of work; without paying much heed to the guards' commands, they divided themselves into teams, rotating the hardest labor. Most of the guards both looked and felt bored, cold, and superfluous; their mood was sullen, as it had been ever since the brief and unfulfilled excitement of raiding the villages and rounding up the men.

The sun came out late in the morning, but by midday the clouds had thickened and the rain was beginning again. Captain Eden ordered a break for a meal—another ration of ruined bread—and was talking with two guards he was sending back to the City to request fresh supplies and some canvas to use for tents and groundcloths, when Lev came over to him.

"One of our people needs a doctor, and two of them are too old for this kind of work." He pointed to Pamplona, who sat, his head bandaged with a torn shirt, talking with Lyons and two gray-headed men. "They should be sent back to their village."

Lev's manner, though not that of an inferior addressing an officer, was perfectly civil. The captain looked at him appraisingly, but not with prejudice. Angel had pointed out this wiry little fellow last night as one of the Shanty Town ringleaders, and it was evident that the villagers tended to look at Lev whenever an order was given or a threat made, as if for direction. How they got it the captain did not know, for he had not seen Lev giving them any orders himself; but if the boy was, in some fashion, a leader, Captain Eden was willing to deal with him as such. The most unnerving element in the situation to the captain was its lack of structure. He was in charge, yet he had no authority beyond what these men, and his own men, were willing to allow him. His men were rough customers at best, and now felt frustrated and ill-used; the Shanty people were an unknown quantity. In the last analysis he had nothing completely dependable except his musket; and nine of his men were also armed.

Whether the odds were thirty against a hundred and twenty, or one against a hundred and forty-nine, the wise course was evidently reasonable firmness without bullying. "It's just a whip cut," he said quietly to the young man. "He can lay off work for a couple of days. The old men can look after the food, dry out this bread, keep the fires going. No one is allowed to leave until the work is done."

"The cut's deep. He'll lose his eye if it isn't looked after. And he's in pain. He has got to go home."

The captain considered. "All right," he said. "If he can't work, he can go. Alone."

"It's too far for him to walk without help."

"Then he stays."

"He'll have to be carried. It'll take four men to carry a stretcher."

Captain Eden shrugged and turned away.

"Senhor, we've agreed not to work until Pamplona's taken care of."

The captain turned to face Lev again, not impatiently, but with a steady gaze. " 'Agreed'—?"

"When he and the old men are sent home, we'll get back to work."

"My orders are from the Council," the captain said, "and your orders are from me. You must make that clear to these men."

"Look," the young man said, with a little warmth but no anger, "we've decided to go ahead, at least temporarily. The work's worth doing, the community does need new farmlands; this is a good location for a village. But we're not obeying orders. We're yielding to your threat of force, in order to spare ourselves, and you, injury or murder. But right now the man whose life's at stake is Pamplona there, and if you won't act to save him, then we have to. The two old men, too; they can't stay here with no shelter. Old Sun has arthritis. Until they're sent home, we can't go on with the work."

Captain Eden's round, swarthy face had gone rather pale. Young Boss Macmilan had told him, "Round up a couple of hundred peasants and get them clearing the west bank of Mill River below the ford," and that had sounded straightforward, not an easy job but a man's job, a real responsibility with reward to follow. But he seemed to be the only one responsible. His men were barely under control, and these Shanty-Towners were incomprehensible. First they were frightened and incredibly meek, now they were trying to give orders to him. If in fact they weren't afraid of his guards, why did they waste time talking? If he was one of them he'd say the hell with it, and make sure he had a machete; they were four to one, and ten at most would be shot before they pulled down and pitchforked the guards who had muskets. There was no sense to their behavior, but it was shameful, unmanly. Where was he to find his own self-respect, in this damned wilderness? The gray river smoking with rain, the tangled, soggy valley, the moldy porridge that was supposed to be bread, the cold down his back where his soaked tunic clung to him, the sullen faces of his men, the voice of this queer boy telling him what to do, it was all too much. He shifted his musket around into his hands. "Listen," he said. "You, and the rest, get back to work. Now. Or I'll have you tied and taken back to the City, to jail. Take your pick."

He had not spoken loudly, but all the others, guards and villagers, were aware of the confrontation. Many stood up from the campfires, knots and clumps of men, mud-blackened, wet hair lank on their foreheads. A while passed, a few seconds, half a minute at most, very long, silent, except for the sound of rain on the raw dirt around them and on the tangled brush sloping down to the river and the leaves of the cotton-wool trees by the river, a fine, soft, vast pattering.

The captain's eyes, trying to watch everything at

once, his men, the villagers, the pile of tools, met Lev's eyes and were held.

"We're stuck, senhor," the young man said almost in a whisper. "What now?"

"Tell them to get to work."

"All right!" Lev said, and turning, "Rolf, Adi, will you start making a stretcher? You and two of the City men will carry Pamplona back to Shantih. Thomas and Sun will go with them. The rest of us back to the job, right?" He and the rest of them went to the pile of hoes and mattocks, picked up their tools, and unhurriedly strung out across the slope again, chopping at the mats of bramble, digging at the roots of shrubs.

Captain Eden, with a cold feeling in the pit of his stomach, turned to his men. The two to whom he had been giving orders stood nearest. "You'll escort the sick ones to their village, before going to the City. And be back with the two able-bodied ones by nightfall. Understand?" He saw Angel, musket in hand, looking at him. "You'll go with them, lieutenant," he said crisply. The two guards, looking blank, saluted; Angel's gaze was openly insolent, jeering.

That evening, by the cooking fire, Lev and three other villagers came to the captain again. "Senhor," said one of the older men, "we've decided, see, that we'll work here for a week, as community labor, if you City men work along with us. It won't do, see, twenty or thirty of you just standing around doing nothing while we work."

"Get these men back where they belong, Martin!" the captain said to a guard on watch duty. The guard lounged forward, hand on whip butt; the villagers looked at one another, shrugged, and returned to their campfire. The important thing, Captain Eden said to himself, was not to talk, not to let them talk. Night came on, black and pouring. It never rained like this in the City; there were roofs there. The noise of the rain was terrible in the darkness, all around, on miles, miles, miles of black wilderness. The fires sputtered, drowned. The guards huddled wretchedly under trees, dropped their musket muzzles in squelching mud, crouched and cursed and shivered. When dawn came, there were no villagers; they had melted off in the night, in the rain. Fourteen guards were also missing.

White-faced, hoarse, defeated, defiant, Captain Eden got his bone-soaked remnant of a troop together and set off back to the City. He would lose his captaincy, perhaps be whipped or mutilated in punishment for his failure, but at the moment he did not care. He did not care for anything they did to him unless it was exile. Surely they would see that it wasn't his fault, nobody could have done this job. Exile was rare, only for the worst crimes, treason, assassination of a Boss; for that men had been driven out of the City, taken by boat far up the coast, marooned there alone in the wilderness, utterly alone, to be tortured and shot if they ever returned to the City, but none ever had; they had died alone, lost, in the terrible uncaring emptiness, the silence. Captain Eden breathed hard as he walked, his eyes searching ahead for the first sight of the roofs of the City.

In the darkness and the heavy rain the villagers had had to keep to the South Road; they would have got lost at once if they had tried to scatter out over the hills. It was difficult enough to keep to the road, which was no more than a track worn by the feet of fishermen and rutted in places by the wheels of lumber carts. They had to go very slowly, groping their way, until the rain thinned and then the light began to grow. Most of them had crept off in the hours after midnight, and by first light they were still little more than halfway home. Despite their fear of pursuit, most stayed on the road, in order to go faster. Lev had gone with the last group to go, and now deliberately held back behind the others. If he saw the guards coming he could shout warning, and the others could scatter off the road into the underbrush. There was no real need for him to do this, all of them were keeping a sharp lookout behind them; but it was an excuse for him to be alone. He didn't want to be with the others, or to talk. He wanted to be by himself, as the wet silver sunrise lifted over the eastern hills; he wanted to walk alone with victory.

They had won. It had worked. They had won their battle without violence. No deaths; one injury. The "slaves" freed without making a threat or striking a blow; the Bosses running back to their Bosses to report failure, and perhaps to wonder why they had failed, and to begin to understand, to see the truth. . . . They were decent enough men, the captain and the others; when they finally got a glimpse of freedom, they would come to it. The City would join the Town, in the end. When their guards deserted them, the Bosses would give up their miserable playing at government, their pretense of power over other men. They too would come, more slowly than the working people, but even they would come to understand that to be free they must put their weapons and defenses down and come outside, equal among equals, brothers. And then indeed the sun would rise over the community of Mankind on Victoria, as now, beneath the heavy masses of the clouds over the hills the silver light broke clear, and every shadow leaped black across the narrow road, and every puddle of last night's rain flashed like a child's laugh.

And it was I, Lev thought with incredulous delight, it was I who spoke for them, I whom they turned to, and I didn't let them down. We held fast! Oh, my God, when he fired that gun in the air, and I thought I was dead, and then I thought I was deaf! But yesterday, with the captain, I never thought "What if he fired?" because I knew he never could have raised the gun, he knew it, the gun wasn't any use. . . . If there's something you must do, you can do it. You can hold fast. I came through, we all came through. Oh, my God, how I love them, love all of them. I didn't know, I didn't know there was such happiness in the world!

He strode on through the bright air toward home, and the fallen rain broke in its quick, cold laughter round his feet.

7

"We need more hostages—especially their leaders, their chiefs. We must anger them into defiance, but not frighten them so much that they're afraid to act. Do you understand? Their defense is passivity and talk, talk, talk. We want them to strike back, while we have their leaders, so their defiance will be disorganized and easily broken. Then they'll be demoralized, easy to work with. You must try to take the boy, what's his name, Shults; the man Elia; anyone else who acts as spokesman. You must provoke them, but stop short of terrifying them. Can you count on your men to stop when you say stop?"

Luz could hear no reply from Herman Macmilan but a careless, grudging mumble. Clearly he did not like being told that he "must" do this and that, nor being asked if he understood.

"Be sure you get Lev Shults. His grandfather was one of their great leaders. We can threaten execution. And carry it out if need be. But it would be better not to. If we frighten them too much they'll fall back on these ideas of theirs, and cling to them because they have nothing else. What we want to do, and it will take restraint on our part, is to force them to betray their ideas—to lose faith in their leaders and their arguments and their talk about peace."

Luz stood outside her father's study, just beneath the window, which was wide open to the windless, rainy air. Herman Macmilan had come stomping into the house a few minutes ago with some news; she had heard his voice, loud in anger and accusation— "We should have used my men in the first place! I told you so!" She was curious to know what had happened, and curious to hear anybody speak in such a tone to her father. But Herman's tirade did not last long. By the time she got outside and under the window where she could eavesdrop, Falco was in full control and Herman was grumbling, "Yes, yes." So much for Bigmouth Macmilan. He had learned who gave the orders in Casa Falco, and in the City. But the orders. . . .

She touched her cheeks, wet with fine rain, and then shook her hands quickly as if she had touched something slimy. Her silver bracelets clinked, and she froze like a coney, pressed up close to the house wall beneath the window so that if Herman or her father looked out they would not see her. Once while Falco was speaking he came and leaned his hands on the sill; his voice was directly above her, and she imagined she could feel the warmth of his body in the air. She felt a tremendous impulse to jump up and shout "Boo!" and at the same time was wildly planning excuses, explanations—"I was looking for a thimble I dropped—" She wanted to laugh aloud, and was listening, listening, with a sense of bewilderment that made tears rise in her throat. Was that her father, her father saying such hideous things? Vera had said that he had a great soul. Would a great soul talk so about tricking people, frightening them, killing them, using them?

That's what he's doing with Herman Macmilan, Luz thought. Using him.

Why not, why not? What else was Herman Macmilan good for?

And what was she good for? To be used, and he had used her—for his vanity, for his comfort, as his pet, all her life; and these days, he used her to keep

Herman Macmilan docile. Last night he had ordered her to entertain Herman with courtesy, whenever he wanted to speak with her. Herman had no doubt complained about her running away from him. Great, whining, complaining bully. Bullies, both of them, all of them, with their big chests and their big boasts and their orders and their cheating plans.

Luz was no longer listening to what the two men were saying. She stepped away from the house wall, standing straight, as if indifferent to any eye that saw her. She walked on around the house to the back entrance, went in through the peaceful, dirty kitchens of siesta time, and to the room that had been given to Vera Adelson.

Vera had been taking siesta too, and received her sleepily.

"I've been eavesdropping on my father and Herman Macmilan," Luz said, standing in the middle of the room, while Vera, sitting on the bed, blinked at her. "They're planning a raid on the Town. They're going to take Lev and all the other leaders prisoner, and then try to make your people get angry and fight, so they can beat them up and send a lot of them to work on the new farms as punishment. They already sent some of them down there, but they all ran away, or the guards ran away—I didn't hear that part clearly. So now Macmilan is going with his 'little army' and my father tells him to force the people to fight back, then they'll betray their ideas and then he can use them as he likes."

Vera sat staring. She said nothing.

"You know what he means. If you don't, Herman does. He means let Herman's men go for the women." Luz' voice was cold, though she spoke very quickly. "You should go warn them."

Vera still said nothing. She gazed at her own bare feet with a remote stare, either dazed or thinking as fast as Luz had been talking.

"Do you still refuse to go? Does your promise still hold you? After that?"

"Yes," the older woman said, faintly, as if absent-mindedly, then more strongly, "yes."

"Then I'm going to go."

"Go where?"

She knew; she asked merely to gain time.

"To warn them," Luz said.

"When is this attack to be?"

"Tomorrow night, I think. In the night, but I wasn't sure which night they meant."

There was a pause.

"Maybe it's tonight. They said, 'It's better if they're in bed.' " It was her father who had said that, it was Herman Macmilan who had laughed.

"And if you go . . . then what will you do?"

Vera still spoke as if sleepy, in a low voice, pausing often.

"I'll tell them, and then come back."

"Here?"

"No one will know. I'll leave word I'm visiting with Eva. That doesn't matter. —If I tell the Town people what I heard, what will they do?"

"I don't know."

"But it would help if they knew, and could plan ahead? You told me how you have to plan what you're going to do, get everybody ready—"

"Yes. It would help. But—"

"Then I'll go. Now."

"Luz. Listen. Think what you're doing. Can you go in broad daylight, and nobody notice you leaving the City? Can you come back? Think—"

"I don't care if I can't come back. This house is full of lies," the girl said in the same cold, quick voice; and she went.

Going was easy. Keeping on going was hard.

To take up an old black shawl as she went out, and wrap herself in it as a raincoat and a disguise; to slip out the back door and up the back street, trotting along like a servant in a hurry to be home; to leave Casa Falco, to leave the City, that was easy. That was exciting. She was not afraid of being stopped; she was not afraid of anybody. If they stopped her all she need say was, "I am the daughter of Councillor Falco!" and they wouldn't dare say a word. No one stopped her. She was quite sure that no one recognized her, for she went by back alleys, the shortest way out of the City, up past the school; the black shawl was over her head, and the rainy sea wind that seemed to blow her on her way blew in the eyes of anyone coming against her. Within a few minutes she was out of the streets, cutting across the back of the Macmilans' lumberyards, among the stacks of logs and planks; then up the bluffs, and she was on the road to Shanty Town.

That was when it began to be hard, when she set her feet on that road. She had only been on it once in her life, when she had gone with a group of her friends, suitably escorted by aunts, duennas, and guards from Casa Marquez, to see the dancing at the Meeting House. It had been summer, they had chattered and laughed all the way, Eva's Aunt Caterina's pedicab had lost a wheel and plumped her down in the dust and all afternoon Aunt Caterina had watched the dancing with a great circle of white dust on the rear of her black dress, so that they couldn't stop giggling. . . . But they had not even gone through the Town. What was it like there? Whom should she ask for, in Shanty Town, and what should she say to them? She should have talked it over with Vera first, instead of rushing out in such a hurry. What would they say to her? Would they even let her in, coming from the City? Would they stare at her, jeer at her, try to hurt her? They were not supposed to hurt anybody. Probably they simply would not talk to her. The wind at her back felt cold now. Rain had soaked through shawl and dress down her back, and the hem of her skirt was heavy with mud and moisture. The fields were empty, gray with autumn. When she looked back there was nothing to be seen but the Monument Tower, pallid and derelict, pointing meaninglessly at the sky; everything she knew now lay hidden behind that marking point. To the left sometimes she glimpsed the river, wide and gray, rain blowing across it in vague gusts.

She would give her message to the first person she

met, let them do what they liked about it; she would
turn straight round and come back home. She would
be back within an hour at most, long before supper-
time.

She saw a small farmhouse off to the left of the road
among orchard trees, and a woman out in the yard.
Luz checked her rapid walk. She would turn aside to
the farm, give the woman her message, then the
woman could go on and tell the people in Shanty
Town, and she could turn back right here and go
home. She hesitated, started toward the farm, then
turned and strode back through the rain-soaked
grasses onto the road again. "I'll just go on and get it
done and come back," she whispered to herself. "Go
on, get it done, come back." She walked faster than
ever, almost running. Her cheeks were burning; she
was out of breath. She had not walked far or fast for
months, years. She must not come in among strangers
all red and gasping. She forced herself to slow her
pace, to walk steadily, erect. Her mouth and throat
were dry. She would have liked to stop and drink the
rain off the leaves of roadside bushes, curling her
tongue to get at the cool drops that beaded every
blade of wild grass. But that would be like a child. It
was a longer road than she had thought. Was she on
the Shanty Town road at all? Had she mistaken the
way and got on some loggers' road, some track with
no end, leading out into the wilderness?

At the word—the wilderness—a cold jolt of terror
went right through her body, stopping her in mid-
step.

She looked back to see the City, the dear narrow

warm crowded beautiful City of walls and roofs and streets and faces and voices, her house, her home, her life, but there was nothing, even the Tower had dropped behind the long rise of the road and was gone. The fields and hills were empty. The vast, soft wind blew from the empty sea.

There's nothing to be afraid of, Luz told herself. Why are you such a coward? You can't get lost, you're on a road, if it's not the Town Road all you have to do is turn back and you'll get home. You won't be climbing so you won't come on a rock scorpion, you won't be in the woods so you won't get into poison rose, what are you so afraid of, there's nothing to hurt you, you're perfectly safe, on the road.

But she walked in terror, her eyes on every stone and shrub and clump of trees, until over the crest of a stony rise she saw red-thatched roofs, and smelled hearth smoke. She came walking into Shanty Town. Her face was set, her back straight; she held the shawl wrapped tight around her.

The small houses stood straggled about among trees and vegetable gardens. There were a lot of houses, but the place wasn't gathered in, walled, protective, like the City. It was all straggling, damp, humble-looking in the quiet, rainy afternoon. There were no people nearby. Luz came slowly down the wandering street, trying to decide—should I call to that man over there? should I knock at this door?

A small child appeared from nowhere in particular and stared at her. He was fair-skinned, but coated with brown mud from toes to knees and fingertips to elbows, with more mud in splotches here and there,

so that he seemed to be a variegated or piebald child.
What clothes he wore were also ringstraked and
spotted with an interesting variety of tones of mud.
"Hello," he said after a long pause, "who are you?"

"Luz Marina. Who are you?"

"Marius," he said, and began to sidle away.

"Do you know where—where Lev Shults lives?"
She did not want to ask for Lev, she would rather face
a stranger; but she could not remember any other
name. Vera had told her about many of them, she had
heard her father mention the "ringleaders'" names,
but she could not remember them now.

"Lev what?" said Marius, scratching his ear and
thus adding a rich deposit to the mudbank there.
Shanty-Towners, she knew, never seemed to use last
names among themselves, only in the City.

"He's young, and he . . ." She didn't know what
Lev was, a leader? a captain? a boss?

"Sasha's house is down there," said the variegated
child, pointing down a muddy, overgrown lane, and
sidled away so effectively that he seemed simply to
become part of the general mist and mud.

Luz set her teeth and walked to the house he had
pointed out. There was nothing to be afraid of. It was
just a dirty little place. The children were dirty and
the people were peasants. She would give her message
to whoever opened the door, then it would be done
and she could go home to the high, clean rooms of
Casa Falco.

She knocked. Lev opened the door.

She knew him, though she had not seen him for
two years. He was half-dressed and disheveled, having

been roused from siesta, staring at her with the luminous, childish stupidity of the half-awake. "Oh," he said, yawning, "where's Andre?"

"I am Luz Marina Falco. From the City."

The luminous stare changed, deepened, he woke up.

"Luz Marina Falco," he said. His dark, thin face flashed into life; he looked at her, past her for her companions, at her again, his eyes charged with feelings—alert, wary, amused, incredulous. "Are you here—with—"

"I came alone. I have a—I have to tell you—"

"Vera," he said. No smile on that flashing face now, but tension, passion.

"Vera is all right. So are the others. It's about you, about the Town. Something happened last night, I don't know what—you know about it—"

He nodded, watching her.

"They're angry, and they're going to come here, I think it's tomorrow night, the men young Macmilan has been training, the bullies, and try and take you and the other leaders prisoner, and then—outrage the others so that they'll fight back, and then they can beat them and make them work on the latifundia for punishment for rebelling. They're coming after dark, tomorrow I think but I'm not sure of that, and he has about forty of them, I think, but all with muskets."

Lev still watched her. He said nothing. Only then, in his silence, did she hear the question she had not asked herself.

And the question took her so off guard, she was so far from the merest beginning of an answer to it, that she stood there and stared back at him, her face growing dull red with bewilderment and fear, and could not say another word.

"Who sent you, Luz?" he asked at last, gently.

It was natural that this should be his answer to the question, that he should think she was lying, or was being used for some kind of trick or spying by Falco. It was natural that he should think that, that he should imagine she was serving her father, and not imagine that she was betraying her father. All she could do was shake her head. Her legs and arms tingled, and there were flashes of light in her eyes; she felt that she was going to be sick. "I have to go back now," she said, but did not move, because her knees would not work.

"Are you all right? Come in, sit down. For a minute."

"I'm dizzy," she said. Her voice sounded thin and whiny, she was ashamed of it. He brought her inside and she sat down in a wicker chair by a table in a dark, long, low-beamed room. She pulled the shawl off her head to get rid of the heat and weight of it; that helped; her cheeks began to cool, and the lights stopped flashing in her eyes as she got used to the dusk of the room. Lev stood near her, at the end of the table. He was barefoot, wearing only trousers; he stood quietly; she could not look at his face, but she sensed in his stance and his quietness no threat, no anger, no contempt.

"I hurried," she said. "I wanted to get back quickly, it's a long way, it made me dizzy." Then she got hold of herself, finding that there was, under the fluster and the fear, a place inside her, a silent corner where her mind could crouch down and think. She thought, and finally spoke again.

"Vera has been living with us. In Casa Falco. You knew that? She and I have been together every day. We talk. I tell her what I hear that's going on, she tells me . . . all kinds of things. . . . I tried to make her come back here. To warn you. She won't, she says she promised not to run away, so she has to keep the promise. So I came. I heard them talking, Herman Macmilan and my father. I listened, I went and stood under the window to listen. What they said made me angry. It made me sick. So when Vera wouldn't come, I came. Do you know about these new guards, Macmilan's guards?"

Lev shook his head, watching, intent.

"I'm not lying," she said coldly. "Nobody is using me. Nobody but Vera even knows I left the house. I came because I'm sick of being used and sick of lies and sick of doing nothing. You can believe me or not. I don't care."

Lev shook his head again, blinking, as if dazzled. "No, I don't— But slow down a little—"

"There isn't time. I have to go back before anybody notices. All right, my father got young Macmilan to train up a troop of other men, Bosses' sons, as a special army, to use against you people. They haven't talked about anything else for two weeks. They're coming here because of whatever it was that happened down in South Valley, and they're supposed to catch you and the other leaders, and then force your people into fighting so you'll betray your idea of peace, of what do you call it, nonviolence. And then you'll fight and you'll lose, because we're better fighters, and anyway we have guns. Do you know Herman Macmilan?"

"By sight, I think," Lev said. He was so utterly different from the man whose name she had just said and whose image filled her mind—the splendid face and muscular body, broad chest, long legs, strong hands, heavy clothing, tunic, trousers, boots, belt, coat, gun, whip, knife. . . . This man was barefoot; she could see the ribs and breastbone under the dark, fine skin of his chest.

"I hate Herman Macmilan," Luz said, less hurriedly, speaking from the small cool place inside her where she could think. "His soul is about the size of a toenail. You should be afraid of him. I am. He likes to hurt people. Don't try to talk to him, the way you people do. He won't listen. He fills up his whole world. All you can do with that kind of man is hit him, or run away from him. I ran away from him.—Do you believe me?" She could ask that, now.

Lev nodded.

She looked at his hands on the chair back; he was gripping the wooden bar tightly; his hands were nerve and bone under the dark skin, strong, fragile.

"All right. I have to go back," she said, and stood up.

"Wait. You should tell this to the others."

"I can't. You tell them."

"But you said you ran away from Macmilan. Now you're going back to him?"

"No! To my father—to my house—"

But he was right. It was the same thing.

"I came to warn you," she said coldly, "because Macmilan was going to trick you, and deserves to be tricked himself. That's all."

But it wasn't enough.

She looked out the open door and saw the lane she would have to walk on, beyond it the street, then the road, then the City and its streets and her house and her father—

"I don't understand," she said. She sat down again, abruptly, because she was shaky again, though not with fear, now, but with anger. "I didn't think. Vera said—"

"What did she say?"

"She said to stop and think."

"Has she—"

"Wait. I have to think. I didn't then, I have to now."

She sat still in the chair for some minutes, her hands clenched in her lap.

"All right," she said. "This is a war, Vera said. I should be— I have betrayed my father's side. Vera is a hostage to the City. I'll have to be a hostage to the Town. If she can't come and go, neither can I. I have to go through with it." Her breath stuck in her throat, making a catching sound at the end of the sentences.

"We don't take hostages, make prisoners, Luz—"

"I didn't say you did. I said I have to stay here. I *choose* to stay here. Will you let me?"

Lev strode off down the room, ducking automatically as he came under the low crossbeam. His shirt had been drying on a chair before the fire; he put it on, went into the back room, came out with his shoes in his hand, sat down at a chair by the table to put them on. "Look," he said, stooping down to get his shoe on, "you can stay here. Anybody can. We don't make anybody go, we don't make anybody stay." He straightened up, looking directly at her. "But what is your father going to think? Even if he believed you were staying here by choice—"

"He wouldn't allow it. He'd come to get me."

"By force."

"Yes, by force. With Macmilan and his little army, no doubt."

"Then you become the pretext for violence they seek. You must go home, Luz."

"For your sake," she said.

She was simply thinking it out, seeing what she had done and what consequences must follow. But Lev sat motionless, a shoe—a muddy, battered, low boot, she noticed—in his hand.

"Yes," he said. "For our sake. You came here for our sake. Now you go back for our sake. And if they find out you've been here—?" There was a pause. "No," he said. "You can't go back. You'd be caught in the lie—yours and theirs. You came *here*. Because of Vera, because of us. You're with us."

"No, I'm not," Luz said, angrily; but the light and warmth in Lev's face bewildered her mind. He spoke so plainly, with such certainty; he was smiling now. "Luz," he said, "remember, when we were in school? You were always—I always wanted to talk to you, I never got up the courage— We did talk once, at sunset, you asked why I wouldn't fight Angel and his crowd. You never were like the other City girls, you didn't fit, you didn't belong. You belong here. The truth matters to you. Do you remember when you got mad at the teacher once, when he said coneys don't hibernate and Timmo tried to tell how he'd found a whole cave of them hibernating and the teacher was going to whip him for being insolent, do you remember?"

"I said I'd tell my father," Luz said in a low voice. She had turned very white.

"You stood up in the class, you said the teacher didn't know the truth and was going to whip Timmo for telling it—you were only about fourteen. Luz, listen, come with me now, we'll go to Elia's house. You can tell them what you told me and we can settle what to do. You can't go back now and be punished, be ashamed! Listen, you can stay with Southwind, she lives outside of town, you can be quiet there. But come with me now, we can't lose time." He reached out his hand to her across the table, that fine, warm hand full of life; she took it, and met his eyes; her eyes filled up with tears. "I don't know what to do," she said, in tears. "You only have one shoe on, Lev."

8

Short as the time was, the entire community must be rallied, brought together, to stand firm together, to hold fast. Indeed haste was in their favor, for, under no pressure, the timorous and halfhearted might fall away; under threat of imminent attack, all were eager to find and keep the center, the strength of the group.

A center there was, and he was in it—was the center, himself, with Andre, Southwind, Martin, Italia, Santha, and all the others, the young, the determined. Vera was not there, and yet was there, in all their decisions, her gentleness and unshakable firmness. Elia was not there; he and Jewel and several others, mostly older people, stood aside, must stand aside, because their will was not the will of the community. Elia had never been strong for the plan of emigration, and now he argued that they had gone too far, the girl must be sent back to her father at once, with a delegation who would "sit down with the Council and talk—if we'll only sit down and talk to each other, there's no need for all this distrust and defiance. . . ."

"Armed men don't sit down and talk, Elia," said old Lyons, wearily.

It was not to Elia that they turned, but to "Vera's people," the young ones. Lev felt the strength of his friends and the whole community, supporting and upholding. It was as if he were not Lev alone, but Lev times a thousand—himself, but himself immensely increased, enlarged, a boundless self mingled with all the other selves, set free, as no man alone could ever be free.

There was scarcely need to take counsel, to explain to people what must be done, the massive, patient resistance which they must set against the City's violence. They knew already, they thought for him and he for them; his word spoke their will.

The girl Luz, the stranger, self-exiled: her presence in Shantih sharpened this sense of perfect community by contrast, and edged it with compassion. They knew why she had come, and they tried to be kind to her. She was alone among them, scared and suspicious, drawing herself up in her pride and her Boss's-daughter arrogance whenever she did not understand. But she did understand, Lev thought, however much her reason might confuse her; she understood with the heart, for she had come to them, trusting.

When he told her that, told her that she was and always had been, in spirit, one of them, one of the People of the Peace, she put on her disdainful look. "I don't even know what these ideas of yours are," she said. But she had, in fact, learned a great deal from Vera; and during these strange, tense, inactive days of waiting for word or attack from the City, while ordinary work was suspended and "Vera's people" were much together, Lev talked with her as often as he could, longing to bring her fully among them, into the center where so much peace and strength was and where one was not alone.

"It's very dull, really," he explained, "a kind of list of rules, just like school. First you do this, next you do that. First you try negotiation and arbitration of the problem, whatever it is, by existing means and institutions. You try to talk it out, the way Elia keeps saying. That step was Vera's group going to talk with the Council, you see. It didn't work. So you go on to step two: noncooperation. A kind of settling down and holding still, so they know you mean what you said. That's where we are now. Then step three, which we're now preparing: issue of an ultimatum. A final appeal, offering a constructive solution, and a clear explanation of what will be done if that solution isn't agreed upon now."

"And what will be done, if they don't happen to agree?"

"Move on to step four. Civil disobedience."

"What's that?"

"A refusal to obey any orders or laws, no matter what, issued by the authority being challenged. We set up our own, parallel, independent authority, and follow our own course."

"Just like that?"

"Just like that," he said smiling. "It worked, you know, over and over again, on Earth. Against all kinds of threats and imprisonments, tortures, attacks. You can read about it, you should read Mirovskaya's *History*—"

"I can't read books," the girl said with her disdainful air. "I tried one once. —If it worked so well, why did you get sent away from Earth?"

"There weren't enough of us. The governments were too big and too powerful. But they wouldn't have sent us off into exile, would they, if they hadn't been afraid of us?"

"That's what my father says about *his* ancestors," Luz remarked. Her eyebrows were drawn down level above her eyes, dark pondering eyes. Lev watched her, stilled for a moment by her stillness, caught by her strangeness. For despite his insistence that she was one of them, she was not; she was not like Southwind, not like Vera, not like any woman he knew. She was different, alien to him. Like the gray heron of the Meeting Pool, there was a silence in her, a silence that drew him, drew him aside, toward a different center.

He was so caught, so held in watching her, that though Southwind said something he did not hear it, and when Luz herself spoke again he was startled, and for a moment the familiar room of Southwind's house seemed strange, an alien place.

"I wish we could forget about all that," she said. "Earth—it's a hundred years ago, a different world, a different sun, what does it matter to us here? We're here, now. Why can't we do things our way? I'm not from Earth. You're not from Earth. This is our world. . . . It ought to have its own name. 'Victoria,' that's stupid, it's an Earth word. We ought to give it its own name."

"What name?"

"One that doesn't mean anything. Ooboo, or Baba. Or call it Mud. It's all mud—if Earth's called 'earth' why can't this one be called 'mud'?" She sounded angry, as she often did, but when Lev laughed she laughed too. Southwind only smiled, but said in her soft voice, "Yes, that's right. And then we could make a world of our own, instead of always imitating what they did on Earth. If there wasn't any violence there wouldn't have to be any nonviolence. . . ."

"Start with mud and build a world," said Lev. "But don't you see, that's what we're doing?"

"Making mudpies," said Luz.

"Building a new world."

"Out of bits of the old one."

"If people forget what happened in the past, they have to do it all over again, they never get on into the future. That's why they kept fighting wars, on Earth. They forgot what the last one was like. We *are* starting fresh. Because we remember the old mistakes, and won't make them."

"Sometimes it seems to me," said Andre, who was sitting on the hearth mending a sandal for Southwind—his side-trade was cobbling—"if you don't mind my saying so, Luz, that in the City they remember all the old mistakes so they can make them all over again."

"I don't know," she said with indifference. She stood up, and went to the window. It was closed, for the rain had not stopped and the weather was colder, with a wind from the east. The small fire in the hearth kept the room warm and bright. Luz stood with her back to that snugness, looking out through the tiny, cloudy panes of the window at the dark fields and the windy clouds.

On the morning after she came to Shantih, after talking with Lev and the others, she had written a letter to her father. A short letter, though it had taken her all morning to write it. She had shown it first to Southwind, then to Lev. When he looked at her now, the straight strong figure outlined black against the light, he saw again the writing of her letter, straight black stiff strokes. She had written:

> Honored Sir!
> I have left our House. I will stay in Shanty Town because I do not approve of Your plans. I decided to leave and I decided to stay. No body is holding me prisoner or hostage. These people are my Hosts. If you mis treat them I am not on Your side. I had to make this choice. You have made a mistake about H. Macmilan. Senhora Adelson had nothing to do with my coming here. It was my Choice.
>   Your respectful Daughter
>   Luz Marina Falco Cooper

No word of affection; no plea for forgiveness.

And no answer. The letter had been taken by a runner at once, young Welcome; he had shoved it under the door of Casa Falco and trotted right on. As soon as he got safe back to Shantih, Luz had begun to wait for her father's response, to dread it but also, visibly, to expect it. That was two full days ago. No answer had come; no attack or assault at night; nothing. They all discussed what change in Falco's plans Luz's defection might have caused, but they did not discuss it in front of her, unless she brought it up.

She said now, "I don't understand your ideas, really. All the steps, all the rules, all the talk."

"They are our weapons," Lev replied.

"But why fight?"

"There's no other choice."

"Yes, there is. To go."

"Go?"

"Yes! Go north, to the valley you found. Just go. Leave. It's what I did," she added, looking imperiously at him when he did not answer at once. "I left."

"And they'll come after you," he said gently.

She shrugged. "They haven't. They don't care."

Southwind made a little noise of warning, protest, sympathy; it really said all that needed saying, but Lev translated it—"But they do, and they will, Luz. Your father—"

"If he comes after me, I'll run farther. I'll go on."

"Where?"

She turned away again and said nothing. They all thought of the same thing: of the wilderness. It was as if the wilderness came into the cabin, as if the walls fell down, leaving no shelter. Lev had been there, Andre had been there, months of the endless, voiceless solitude; it was in their souls now and they could never wholly leave it. Southwind had not been in the wilderness, but her love lay buried in it. Even Luz who had never seen or known it, the child of those who for a hundred years had built up their walls against it and denied it, knew it and feared it, knew it was foolishness to talk of leaving the Colony, alone. Lev watched her in silence. He pitied her, sharp pity, as for a hurt, stubborn child who refuses comfort, holds aloof, will not weep. But she was not a child. It was a woman he saw standing there, a woman standing alone in a place without help or shelter, a woman in the wilderness; and pity was lost in admiration and in fear. He was afraid of her. There was a strength in her that was not drawn from love or trust or community, did not rise from any source that should give strength, any source he recognized. He feared that strength, and craved it. These three days he had been with her, he had thought of her constantly, had seen everything in terms of her: as if all their struggle made sense only if she could be made to understand it, as if her choice outweighed their plans and the ideals they lived by. —She was pitiable, admirable, precious as any human soul was precious, but she must not take over his mind. She must be one of them, acting with him, supporting him, not filling and confusing his thoughts like this. Later, there would be time to think about her and understand her, when the confrontation was over, when they had won through to peace. Later, there would be all the time in the world.

"We can't go north now," he said patiently, a little coldly. "If a group left now, it would weaken the unity of those who must stay behind. And the City would track settlers down. We have to establish our freedom to go—here, now. Then we will go."

"Why did you give them the maps, show them the way!" Luz said, impatiently and hotly. "That was stupid. You could have just *gone*."

"We are a community," Lev said, "the City and the Town." And left it at that.

Andre rather spoiled his point by adding, "Anyhow, we couldn't just sneak off. A big lot of people migrating leave a very easy trail to follow."

"So if they did follow you all the way north there to your mountains—you're there already, and you say, Too bad, this is ours, go find yourselves another valley, there's plenty of room!"

"And they would use force. The principle of equality and free choice must be established first. Here."

"But they use force here! Vera's already a prisoner, and the others in the Jail, and the old man lost his eye, and the bullies are coming to beat you up or shoot you—all to establish a 'principle,' when you could have gone, got out, gone free!"

"Freedom's won by sacrifice," Southwind said. Lev looked at her, then quickly at Luz; he was not sure if Luz knew of Timmo's death on the journey to the north. Probably, here alone with Southwind the last three nights, she did. In any case, the quietness of Southwind's voice quieted her. "I know," Luz said. "You have to take risks. But sacrifice. . . . I hate that idea, sacrifice!"

Lev grinned in spite of himself. "And what have you done?"

"Not sacrificed myself for any idea! I just ran away—don't you understand? And that's what you all ought to do!" Luz spoke in challenge, defiance, self-defense, not conviction; but Southwind's response startled Lev. "You may be right," she said. "So long as we stand and fight, even though we fight with our weapons, we fight their war."

Luz Falco was an outsider, a stranger, she did not know how the People of the Peace thought and felt,

but to hear Southwind say something irresponsible
was shocking, an affront to their perfect unity.

"To run away and hide in the forest—that's a
choice?" Lev said. "For coneys, yes. Not for human
beings. Standing upright and having two hands
doesn't make us human. Standing up and having ideas
and ideals does! And holding fast to those ideals. Together. We can't live alone. Or we die alone—like
animals."

Southwind nodded sadly, but Luz frowned straight
back at him. "Death is death, does it matter whether
it's in bed in the house or outside in the forest? We
are animals. That's why we die at all."

"But to live and die for—for the sake of the spirit
—that's different, that's different from running and
hiding, all separate, selfish, scratching for food, cower-
ing, hating, each alone—" Lev stammered, he felt his
face hot. He met Luz's eyes, and stammered again,
and was silent. Praise was in her look, praise such as
he had never earned, never dreamed of earning, praise
and rejoicing, so that he knew himself confirmed, in
that same moment of anger and argument, confirmed
totally, in his words, his life, his being.

This is the true center, he thought. The words went
quick and clear across his mind. He did not think of
them again, but nothing, on the far side of those
words, was the same; nothing would ever be the same.
He had come up into the mountains.

His right hand was half held out toward Luz in a
gesture of urgent pleading. He saw it, she saw it,
that unfinished gesture. Suddenly self-conscious, he

dropped his hand; the gesture was unfinished. She moved abruptly, turning away, and said with anger and despair, "Oh, I don't understand, it's all so strange, I'll never understand, you know everything and I've never even thought about anything. . . ." She looked physically smaller as she spoke, small, furious, surrendering. "I just wish—" She stopped short.

"It will come, Luz," he said. "You don't have to run to it. It comes, it will come—I promise—"

She did not ask what he promised. Nor could he have said.

When he left the house the rainy wind struck him in the face, taking his breath away. He gasped; tears filled his eyes, but not from the wind. He thought of that bright morning, the silver sunrise and his great happiness, only three days ago. Today it was gray, no sky, little light, a lot of rain and mud. Mud, the world's name is Mud, he thought, and wanted to laugh, but his eyes were still full of tears. She had renamed the world. That morning on the road, he thought, that was happiness, but this is—and he had no word for it, only her name, Luz. Everything was contained in that, the silver sunrise, the great burning sunset over the City years ago, all the past, and all that was to come, even their work now, the talking and the planning, the confrontation, and their certain victory, the victory of the light. "I promise, I promise," he whispered into the wind. "All my life, all the years of my life."

He wanted to walk slower, to stop, to hold the moment. But the very wind that blew in his face forced him forward. There was so much to do, so

little time now. Later, later! Tonight might be the
night Macmilan's gang came; there was no knowing.
Evidently, guessing that Luz had betrayed their plan,
they had changed it. There was nothing to do, until
their own plans were complete, but wait and be ready.
Readiness was all. There would be no panic. No
matter whether City or Town made the first move,
the People of the Peace would know what to do, how
to act. He strode on, almost running, into Shantih.
The taste of the rain was sweet on his lips.

He was at home, late in the dark afternoon, when
the message came. His father brought it from the
Meeting House. "A scar-faced fellow, a guard," Sasha
said in his soft ironic voice. "Came strolling up, asked
for Shults. I think he meant you, not me."

It was a note on the thick, coarse paper they made
in the City. For a moment Lev thought Luz had
written the stiff black words—

> Shults: I will be at the smelting ring at
> sundown today. Bring as many as you like.
> I will be alone.
>   Luis Burnier Falco

A trick, an obvious trick. Too obvious? There was
just time to get back to Southwind's house and show
Luz the note.

"If he says he'll be there alone, he'll be alone," she
said.

"You heard him planning to trick us, with Macmilan," Andre said.

She glanced past Andre with contempt. "This is his name," she said. "He wouldn't put his name to a lie. He'll be there alone."

"Why?"

She shrugged.

"I'm going," Lev said. "Yes! With you, Andre! And as many as you think necessary. But you'll have to round them up pretty quick. There's only an hour or so of daylight left."

"You know they want you as a hostage," Andre said. "Are you going to walk right into their hands?"

Lev nodded energetically. "Like a wotsit," he said, and laughed. "In—and out! Come on, let's get a bunch together, Andre. Luz—do you want to come?"

She stood indecisive.

"No," she said; she winced. "I can't. I'm afraid."

"You're wise."

"I should go. To tell him myself that you're not keeping me here, that I chose. He doesn't believe it."

"What you choose, and whether he believes it, doesn't really matter," Andre said. "You're still a pretext: their property. Better not come, Luz. If you're there they'll probably use force to get you back."

She nodded, but still hesitated. Finally she said, "I should come." She said it with such desperate resolution that Lev broke in, "No—" but she went on: "I have to. I won't stand aside and be talked about, fought over, handed back and forth."

"You will not be handed back," Lev said. "You belong to yourself. Come with us if you choose."

She nodded.

The smelting ring was an ancient ringtree site, south

of the Road halfway between Town and City, and
centuries older than either; the trees had long ago
fallen and decayed, leaving only the round central
pond. The City's first iron-smelting works had been
set up there; it too had decayed, when richer ore was
found in the South Hills forty years ago. The chimneys
and machinery were gone, the old sheds, rotten-
planked and crazy, overgrown with bindweed and
poison rose, crouched abandoned by the flat shore of
the pond.

Andre and Lev had got together a group of twenty
as they came. Andre led them around by the old sheds,
to make sure no party of guards was hiding in or
behind them. They were empty, and there was no
other place for a gang to conceal themselves within
several hundred meters; it was a flat place, treeless,
desolate and miserable-looking in the gloomy end of
the daylight. Fine rain fell onto the round gray water
that lay unsheltered, defenseless, like a blind, open
eye. On the far side of the pond Falco stood waiting
for them. They saw him move away from a thicket
where he had taken some shelter from the rain, and
come walking around the shore to them, alone.

Lev started forward from the others. Andre let him
go ahead, but followed a couple of meters behind
him, with Sasha, Martin, Luz, and several others. The
rest of their group stayed scattered out along the
gray pond's edge and on the slope that led up to the
Road, on guard.

Falco stopped, facing Lev. They stood right on the
shore of the pond, where the walking was easier. Between them lay a tiny muddy inlet of the water, a

bay no wider than the length of a man's arm, with shores of fine sand, a harbor for a child's toy boat. In the intense vividness of his perceptions Lev was as aware of that bit of water and sand, and of how a child might play there, as he was of Falco's erect figure, his handsome face that was Luz's face and yet wholly different, his belted coat darkened by rain on the shoulders and sleeves.

Falco certainly saw his daughter in the group behind Lev, but he did not look at her nor speak to her; he spoke to Lev, in a soft dry voice, a little hard to hear over the vast whisper of the rain.

"I'm alone, as you see, and unarmed. I speak for myself alone. Not as Councillor."

Lev nodded. He felt a desire to call this man by his name, not Senhor or Falco, but his own name, Luis; he did not understand the impulse, and did not speak.

"I wish my daughter to come home."

Lev indicated, with a slight open gesture, that she was there behind him. "Speak to her, Senhor Falco," he said.

"I came to speak to you. If you speak for the rebels."

"Rebels? Against what, senhor? I, or any of us, will speak for Shantih, if you like. But Luz Marina can speak for herself."

"I did not come to argue," Falco said. His manner was perfectly controlled and polite, his face rigid. The quietness, the stiffness were those of a man in pain. "Listen. There is to be an attack on the Town. You know that, now. I could not prevent it, now, if I wanted to, though I have delayed it. But I want my daughter out of it. Safe. If you'll send her home with me, I'll send Senhora Adelson and the other hostages, under guard, to you tonight. I'll come with them, if you like; let her go back with me then. This is between us alone. The rest of it, the fighting—you started it by your disobedience, I cannot stop it, neither can you, now. This is all we can do. Trade our hostages, and so save them."

"Senhor, I respect your candor—but I didn't take Luz Marina from you, and I can't give her back."

As he spoke, Luz came up beside him, wrapped in her black shawl. "Father," she said in a clear, hard voice, not softly as he and Falco had spoken, "you can stop Macmilan's bullies if you want to."

Falco's face did not change; could not change, perhaps, without going to pieces. There was a long silence, full of the sound of rain. The light was heavy, bright only low and far away in the west.

"I can't, Luz," he said in that painful quiet voice. "Herman is—he is determined to take you back."

"And if I came back with you, so that he had no pretext, would you order him not to attack Shantih?"

Falco stood still. He swallowed, hard, as if his throat were very dry. Lev clenched his hands, seeing that, seeing the man stand there in his pride that could endure no humiliation and was humiliated, his strength that must admit to impotence.

"I can't. Things have gone too far." Falco swallowed again, and tried again. "Come home with me, Luz Marina," he said. "I will send the hostages back at once. I give my word." He glanced at Lev, and his white face said for him what he could not say, that he asked Lev's help.

"Send them!" Luz said. "You have no right to keep them prisoner."

"And you'll come——" It was not quite a question.

She shook her head. "You have no right to keep me prisoner."

"Not a prisoner, Luz, you are my daughter——" He stepped forward. She stepped back.

"No!" she said. "I will *not* come when you bargain for me. I will never come back so long as you attack and, and p-persecute people!" She stammered and groped for words. "I'll never marry Herman Macmilan, or look at him, I de——I detest him! I'll come when I'm free to come and do what I choose to do and so long as he comes to Casa Falco I will never come home!"

"Macmilan?" the father said in agony. "You don't have to marry Macmilan——" He stopped, and looked from Luz to Lev, a little wildly. "Come home," he said. His voice shook, but he struggled for control. "I will stop the attack if I can. We——we'll talk, with you," he said to Lev. "We'll talk."

"We'll talk now, later, whenever you want," Lev said. "It's all we ever asked, senhor. But you must not ask your daughter to trade her freedom for Vera's, or for your goodwill, or for our safety. That is wrong. You can't do it; we won't accept it."

Again Falco stood still, but it was a different stillness: defeat, or his final refusal of defeat? His face, white and wet with rain or sweat, was set, inexpressive.

"Then you will not let her go," he said.

"I will not come," Luz answered.

Falco nodded once, turned, and walked slowly away

along the curving shore of the pond. He passed the thickets that stood blurred and shapeless in the late twilight, and set off up the slight slope to the road that led back to the City. His straight, short, dark figure was quickly lost to sight.

9

One of the servant girls tapped at Vera's door, opened it, and said in the half-impertinent, half-timid voice the maids used when "following orders," "Senhora Vera, Don Luis will see you in the big room, please!"

"Oh dear, oh dear," Vera sighed. "Is he still in a bad mood?"

"Terrible," the girl, Teresa, said, at once dropping her "following orders" manner and stooping to scratch a callus on her hard, bare, plump foot. Vera was by now considered a friend, a kind of good luck aunt or elder sister, by all the house girls; even the stern middle-aged cook Silvia had come to Vera's room the day after Luz's disappearance, and had discussed it with her, apparently not caring in the least that she was seeking reassurance from the enemy. "Have you seen Michael's face?" Teresa went on. "Don Luis knocked two of his teeth loose yesterday because Michael was slow taking off his boots, he was grunting and groaning, you know how he does everything, and Don Luis just went whack! with his foot with the boot still on. Now Michael's all swelled up like a pouchbat, he does look funny. Linda says that Don Luis went to

Shanty Town yesterday evening all by himself, Marquez's Thomas saw him, he was going right up the road. What do you think happened? Was he trying to steal poor Senhorita Luz back, do you think?"

"Oh dear," Vera sighed again. "Well, I'd better not keep him waiting." She smoothed her hair, straightened her clothes, and said to Teresa, "What pretty earrings you have on. Come on!" And she followed the girl to the hall of Casa Falco.

Luis Falco was sitting in the deep window seat, gazing out over Songe Bay. A restless morning light lay on the sea; the clouds were big, turbulent, their crests dazzling white as the sun flashed out on them, dark when the wind flawed and higher clouds veiled the light. Falco stood up to meet Vera. His face looked hard and very weary. He did not look at her as he spoke. "Senhora, if you have any belongings here you wish to take with you, please get them."

"I have nothing," Vera said slowly. Falco had never frightened her before; indeed, in her month in his house, she had come to like him very much, to honor him. There was a change in him now; not the pain and rage that had been visible, and understandable, since Luz's flight; not an emotion, but a change in the man, an evidence of destruction, as in one deathly ill or injured. She sought somehow to reach him, and did not know how. "You gave me clothes, Don Luis, and all the rest," she said. The clothes she wore now had been his wife's, she knew that; he had had a chest of clothing brought to her room, beautiful fine-woven skirts and blouses and shawls, all folded away carefully, leaves of the sweet lavender scattered among them so long ago that all their scent was gone. "Shall I go change to my own things?" she asked.

"No. —Yes, if you wish. As you like. —Come back here as quickly as possible, please."

When she returned in five minutes, in her own suit of white treesilk, he was again sitting motionless in the window seat, gazing out over the great silver cloud-hung bay.

Again he rose when she approached him, again he did not look at her. "Come with me, please, senhora."

"Where are you going?" Vera asked, not moving.

"To the Town." He added, as if he had forgotten to mention it, thinking of something entirely different, "I hope it will be possible for you to rejoin your people there."

"I hope so too. What would make it impossible, Don Luis?"

He did not answer. She felt that he was not evading her question, only that the labor of answering it was beyond him. He stood aside for her to precede him. She looked around the big room that she had come to know so well, and at his face. "I will thank you now for your kindness to me, Don Luis," she said with formality. "I will remember the true hospitality, that made a prisoner a guest."

His tired face did not change; he shook his head, and waited for her.

She passed him, and he followed her through the hall and out onto the street. She had not set foot across that doorway since the day she was brought to the house.

She had hoped that Jan and Hari and the others might be there, but there was no sign of them. A dozen men, whom she recognized as Falco's personal guards and servants, were waiting in a group, and there was another group of middle-aged men, among them Councillor Marquez and Falco's brother-in-law Cooper, with some of their retinue, perhaps thirty in all. Falco looked them all over with a rapid glance, then, still with mechanical deference to Vera, letting her precede him by a step, set off down the steep street, with a gesture to the others to follow him.

As they walked she heard old Marquez talking to Falco, but did not hear what they said. Scarface, Anibal, gave her the faintest shadow of a wink as he stepped smartly by with his brother. The force and brightness of the wind and sunlight, after so long indoors or in the walled garden of the house, bewildered her; she felt unsteady walking, as if she had been sick in bed a long time.

In front of the Capitol a larger group was waiting, about forty men, perhaps fifty, all of them fairly young, all of them wearing the same kind of coat, a heavy blackish-brown material; the cottonwool mills must have worked overtime to make so much cloth all the same, Vera thought. The coats were belted and had big metal buttons, so that they all looked pretty much alike. All the men had both whips and muskets. They looked like one of the murals inside the Capitol. Herman Macmilan stepped forward from among them, tall, broad-shouldered, smiling. "At your service, Don Luis!"

"Good morning, Don Herman. All ready?" Falco said in his stifled voice.

"All ready, senhor. To the Town, men!" And he swung round and led the column of men straight up Seaward Street, not waiting for Falco, who took Vera by the arm and hurried forward with her among the dark-coated men to join Macmilan at the head of the troop. His own followers tried to press in behind him. Vera was jostled among the men, their guns and whipstocks, their hard arms, their faces glancing down at her, young and hostile. The street was narrow and Falco shoved his way by main force, pulling Vera along with him. But the instant he came out abreast of Macmilan at the head of the troop he let go Vera's arm and walked sedately, as if he had been there at the head all along.

Macmilan glanced at him and smiled, his usual tight, pleased smile. He then pantomimed surprise at the sight of Vera. "Who is that, Don Luis? Have you brought a duenna along?"

"Any more reports of the Town this last hour?"

"Still gathering; not on the move yet, at last report."

"The City Guard will meet us at the Monument?"

The young man nodded. "With some reinforcements Angel rounded up. High time we got moving! These men have been kept waiting too long."

"They're your men, I expect you to keep them in order," Falco said.

"They're so keen for action," Macmilan said with pretended confidentiality. Vera saw Falco shoot him one quick, black glance.

"Listen, Don Herman. If your men won't take orders—if you won't take orders—then we stop here: now." Falco stopped, and the force of his personality was such that Vera, Macmilan, and the men behind them stopped with him, as if they were all tied to him on one string.

Macmilan's smile was gone. "You are in command, Councillor," he said, with a flourish that did not hide the sullenness beneath.

Falco nodded and strode on. It was now he who set the pace, Vera noticed.

As they approached the bluffs she saw at the top, near the Monument, a still larger body of men waiting for them; and when they reached the top and passed under the shadow of the spectral, dingy space ship, this troop joined in behind Falco's men and Macmilan's browncoats, so that as they went on along the Road there were two hundred or more of them.

But what are they doing? Vera thought. Is this the attack on Shantih? But why would they bring me? What are they going to do? Falco is mad with pain and Macmilan is mad with envy, and then these men, all these men, all so big, with their guns and their coats and striding along like this, I can't keep up, if only Hari and the others were here so I could see a human face! Why have they brought only me, where are the other hostages, have they killed them? They're all mad, you can smell them, they smell like blood— Do they know they're coming, in Shantih? Do they know? What will they do? Elia! Andre! Lev my dear! What are you going to do, what are you going to do?

Can you hold fast? I can't keep up, they walk so fast, I can't keep up.

Though the people of Shantih and the villages had begun gathering—for the Short March, as Sasha unsmilingly described it—early in the morning, they did not get under way until nearly noon; and being a large crowd, unwieldy, and rendered somewhat chaotic by the presence of many children and by the constant arrival of stragglers seeking for friends to walk with, they did not move very quickly down the road toward the City.

Falco and Macmilan, on the contrary, had moved very quickly when they were brought word of a great massing of Shanty-Towners on the road. They had their troop—Macmilan's army, City Guards, the private bodyguards of several Bosses, and a mixed lot of volunteers—out on the Road by noon, and moving fast.

So the two groups met on the road at Rocktop Hill, closer to the Town than to the City. The vanguard of the People of the Peace came over the low crest of the hill and saw the City men just starting up the rise toward them. They halted at once. They had the advantage of superior height where they stood, but a disadvantage too, in that most of them were still on the eastern side of the hill, and so could not see what was going on, nor be seen. Elia suggested to Andre and Lev that they withdraw a hundred meters or so, to meet the City on equal footing at the hilltop; and though this withdrawal might be construed as yielding or weakness, they decided it was best. It was worth it to see Herman Macmilan's face when he swaggered up to the hilltop and saw for the first time what he was facing: some four thousand people massed along the road down the whole slope of the hill and far back along the flat, children and women and men, the greatest gathering of human beings ever to take place on that world; and they were singing. Macmilan's ruddy face lost its color. He gave some order to his men, the ones in brown coats, and they all did something with their guns, and then held them ready in their hands. Many of the guards and volunteers began yelling and shouting to drown out the singing, and it was some while before they could be brought to silence so that the leaders of the two groups could speak.

Falco had begun speaking, but there was still a lot of noise, and his dry voice did not carry. Lev stepped forward and took the word from him. His voice silenced all others, ringing out in the silvery, windy air of the hilltop, jubilant.

"The People of the Peace greet the representatives of the City in comradeship! We have come to explain to you what we intend to do, what we ask you to do, and what will happen if you reject our decisions. Listen to what we say, people of Victoria, for all our hope lies in this! First, our hostages must be set free. Second, there will be no further forced-work drafts. Third, representatives from Town and City will meet to set up a fairer trade agreement. Finally, the Town's plan to found a colony in the north will proceed without interference from the City, as the City's plan to open South Valley along the Mill River to settlement will proceed without interference from the Town. These four points have been discussed and agreed upon by all the people of Shantih, and they are not subject to negotiation. If they are not accepted by the Council, the people of Shantih must warn the people of the City that all cooperation in work, all trade, all furnishing of food, wood, cloth, ores, and products will cease and will not be resumed until the four points are accepted and acted upon. This resolve is not open to compromise. We will in no case use violence against you; but until our demands are met we will in no way cooperate with you. Nor will we bargain with you, or compromise. I speak the conscience of my people. We will hold fast."

So surrounded by the big brown-coated men that she could see nothing but shoulders and backs and gun stocks, Vera stood trembling, still badly out of breath from the hurried march, and blinking back tears. The clear, courageous, strong, young voice, speaking without anger or uncertainty, singing the words of reason and of peace, singing Lev's soul, her soul, their soul, the challenge and the hope—

"There is no question," said the dark dry voice, Falco's voice, "of bargaining or compromise. On that we agree. Your show of numbers is impressive. But bear in mind, all of you, that we stand for the law, and that we are armed. I do not wish there to be violence. It is unnecessary. It is you who have forced it on us, by bringing out so large a crowd to force your demands on us. This is intolerable. If your people attempt to advance one step farther toward the City, our men will be ordered to stop them. The responsibility for injuries or deaths will be yours. You have forced us to take extreme measures in defense of the Community of Man on Victoria. We will not hesitate to take them. I will presently give the order to this crowd to disperse and go home. If they do not obey at once, I will order my men to use their weapons at will. Before that, I wish to exchange hostages, as we agreed. The two women, Vera Adelson and Luz Marina Falco, are here? Let them cross the line between us in safety."

"We agreed to no exchange!" Lev said, and now there was anger in his voice.

Herman Macmilan had forced his way among his men and seized Vera by the arm, as if to prevent her escape, or perhaps to escort her forward. That heavy grip on her arm shocked and enraged her, and she trembled again, but she did not pull away, or say anything to Macmilan. She could see both Lev and Falco now, and she stood still.

Lev stood facing her, some ten meters away on the level hilltop. His face looked extraordinarily bright in the restless, flashing sunlight. Elia stood beside him, and was saying something to him hurriedly. Lev shook his head and faced Falco again. "No agreement was made, none will be made. Let Vera and the others free. Your daughter is already free. We do not make bargains, do you understand? And we do not heed threats."

There was no sound now among the thousands of people standing back along the road. Though they could not all hear what was said, the silence had swept back among them; only there was, here and there, a little babbling and whimpering of babies, fretting at being held so tight. The wind on the hilltop gusted hard and ceased. The clouds above Songe Bay were massing heavier, but had not yet hidden the high sun.

Still Falco did not answer.

He turned at last, abruptly. Vera saw his face, rigid as iron. He gestured towards her, to her, unmistakably, to come forward—to come free. Macmilan let go her arm. Incredulous, she took a step forward, a second step. Her eyes sought Lev's eyes; he was smiling. Is it so easy, victory? so easy?

The explosion of Macmilan's gun directly beside her head jerked her whole body backward as if with the recoil of the gun itself. Off balance, she was knocked sideways by the rush of the brown-coated men, then knocked down on hands and knees. There was a crackling, snapping noise and a roaring and high hissing screaming like a big fire, but all far away, where could a fire be burning, here there were only men crushing and crowding and trampling and stumbling; she crawled and cowered, trying to hide, but there was no hiding place, there was nothing left but the hiss of fire, the trampling feet and legs, the crowding bodies, and the sodden stony dirt.

There was a silence, but not a real silence. A stupid meaningless silence inside her own head, inside her right ear. She shook her head to shake the silence out of it. There was not enough light. The sunlight had gone. It was cold, the wind was blowing cold, but it made no sound blowing. She shivered as she sat up, and held her arms against her belly. What a stupid place to fall down, to lie down; it made her angry. Her good suit of treesilk was muddy and blood-soaked, clammy against her breasts and arms. A man was lying down next to her. He wasn't a big man at all. They had all looked so big when they were standing up and crowding her along, but lying down he was quite thin, and he was trampled into the ground as if he was trying to become part of it, half gone back to mud already. Not a man at all anymore, just mud and hair and a dirty brown coat. Not a man at all anymore. Nobody left. She was cold sitting there, and it was a stupid place to sit; she tried to crawl a little. There was nobody left to knock her down, but she still could not get up and walk. From now on she would always have to crawl. Nobody could stand up anymore. There was nothing to hold onto. Nobody could walk. Not anymore. They all lay down on the ground, the few that were left. She found Lev after she had crawled for a while. He was not so trampled into the mud and dirt as the brown-coated man; his face was there, the dark eyes open looking up at the sky; but not looking. There was not enough light left. No light at all anymore, and the wind made no sound. It was going to rain soon, the clouds were heavy overhead like a roof. One of Lev's hands had been trampled, and the bones were broken and showing white. She dragged herself a little farther to a place where she did not have to see that, and took his other hand in her own. It was unhurt, only cold. "So," she said, trying to find some words to comfort him. "So,

there, Lev my dear." She could barely hear the words
she said, way off in the silence. "It will be all right
soon, Lev."

10

"It's all right," Luz said. "Everything is going well.
Don't worry." She had to speak loudly, and she felt
foolish, always saying the same thing; but it always
worked, for a while. Vera would lie back and be
quiet. But presently she would be trying to sit up
again, asking what was happening, anxious and
frightened. She would ask about Lev: "Is Lev all
right? His hand was hurt." Then she would say she
had to go back to the City, to Casa Falco. She should
never have come with those men with the guns, it was
her fault, for wanting so badly to come home. If she
went back to being a hostage again things would go
better, wouldn't they? "Everything is all right, don't
worry," Luz said, loudly, for Vera's hearing had been
damaged. "Everything is going well."

And indeed people went to bed at night and got up
in the morning, did the work, cooked meals and ate
them, talked together; everything went on. Luz went
on. She went to bed at night. It was hard to get to
sleep, and when she slept she woke up in the black
dark from a horrible crowd of pushing, screaming
people; but none of that was happening. It had happened. The room was dark and silent. It had happened, it was over, and everything went on.

The funeral of the seventeen who had been killed was held two days after the march to the City; some were to be buried in their own villages, but the meeting and service for all of them was held at the Meeting House. Luz felt that she did not belong there, and that Andre and Southwind and the others would find it easier if she did not come with them. She said she would stay with Vera, and they left her. But when a long time had passed in the utter silence of the house in the rainswept fields, Vera asleep, Luz picking the seeds from silktree fiber to be doing something with her hands, a man came to the door, a slight, gray-haired man; she did not recognize him at first. "I am Alexander Shults," he said. "Is she asleep? Come on. They shouldn't have left you here." And he took her back with him to the Meeting House, to the end of the service for the dead, and on to the burial ground, in the silent procession that bore the twelve coffins of the dead from Shantih. So she stood in her black shawl in the rain at the graveside by Lev's father. She was grateful to him for that, though she said nothing to him, nor he to her.

She and Southwind worked daily in Southwind's potato field, for the crop had to be got in; another few days and it would begin to rot in the wet ground. They worked together when Vera was asleep, and took turns, one in the field and one in the house, when she was wakeful and needed someone with her. Southwind's mother was often there, and the big, silent, competent Italia, Southwind's friend; and Andre came by once a day, though he too had field-work and also had to spend time daily at the Meeting

House with Elia and the others. Elia was in charge, it was Elia who talked with the City men now. Andre told Luz and Southwind what had been done and said; he expressed no opinion; Luz did not know if he approved or disapproved. All the opinions, beliefs, theories, principles, all that was gone, swept away, dead. The heavy, defeated grief of the great crowd at the funeral service was all that was left. Seventeen people of Shantih dead, there on the Road; eight people of the City. They had died in the name of peace, but they had also killed in the name of peace. It had all fallen apart. Andre's eyes were dark as coals. He joked to cheer up Southwind (and Luz saw, as she saw everything now, dispassionately, that he had been in love with Southwind for a long time), and both girls smiled at his jokes, and tried to make him rest for a while, there with them and Vera. Luz and Southwind worked together, afternoons in the fields. The potatoes were small, firm, and clean, pulling up out of the mud on their fine-tangled tracery of roots. There was a pleasure in the fieldwork; not much in anything else.

From time to time Luz thought, "None of this is happening," for it seemed to her that what did happen was only a kind of picture or screen, like a shadow-play, behind which lay whatever was real. This was a puppet show. It was all so strange, after all. What was she doing in a field in the late afternoon in a misty dark drizzle, wearing patched trousers, mud to the thighs and elbows, pulling potatoes for Shanty Town? All she had to do was get up and walk home. Her blue skirt and the embroidered blouse would be hanging clean and pressed in the closet in her dressing room; Teresa would bring hot water for a bath. There would be big logs in the fireplace at the west end of the hall of Casa Falco, in this weather, and a clear fire burning. Outside the thick glass of the windows the evening would darken bluer and bluer over the Bay. The doctor might drop in for a chat, with his crony Valera, or old Councillor Di Giulio hoping for a game of chess with her father—

No. Those were the puppets, little bright mind-puppets. That was nowhere; this was here: the potatoes, the mud, Southwind's soft voice, Vera's swollen, discolored face, the creaking of the straw mattress in the loft of this hut in Shanty Town in the black dark and stillness of the night. It was strange, it was all wrong, but it was all that was left.

Vera was improving. The physician, Jewel, said the effect of the concussion had worn off; she must stay in bed at least a week longer, but she would be all right. She asked for something to do. Southwind gave her a great basket of cottonwool, gathered from wild trees over in Red Valley, to spin.

Elia came to the door. The three women had just had their noon dinner. Southwind was washing up, Luz was straightening the table, Vera was sitting up against her pillow tying a starter-thread on the spindle. Elia looked clean, like the little potatoes, Luz thought, with his firm round face and blue eyes. His voice was unexpectedly deep, but very gentle. He sat at the cleared table and talked, mostly to Vera. "Everything is going well," he told her. "Everything is all right."

Vera said little. The left side of her face was still misshapen and bruised where she had been kicked or clubbed, but she tilted that side forward in order to hear; her right eardrum had been broken. She sat up against her pillow, set her spindle whirling, and nodded as Elia talked. Luz did not pay much heed to what he said. Andre had told them already: the hostages had been freed; terms of cooperation between City and Town agreed upon, and a fairer exchange in tools and dried fish for the food supplied by the Town; now they were discussing a plan for the joint settlement of the South Valley—work parties from the City opening up the land, then volunteer colonists from the Town moving there to farm.

"And the northern colony?" Vera asked in her quiet thin voice.

Elia looked down at his hands. Finally he said, "It was a dream."

"Was it all a dream, Elia?"

Vera's voice had changed; Luz, putting away the bowls, listened.

"No," the man said. "No! But too much, too soon— too fast, Vera. Too much staked rashly on an act of open defiance."

"Would covert defiance have been better?"

"No. But confrontation was wrong. Cooperation, talking together—reasoning—*reason*. I told Lev— All along, I tried to say—"

There were tears in Elia's blue eyes, Luz noticed. She stacked the bowls neatly in the cupboard and sat down by the hearth.

"Councillor Marquez is a reasonable man. If only he

had been Chief of the Council—" Elia checked himself. Vera said nothing.

"It's Marquez you mostly talk with now, Andre says," said Luz. "Is he Chief of the Council now?"

"Yes."

"Is my father in jail?"

"Under house arrest, they call it," Elia replied, with extreme embarrassment. Luz nodded, but Vera was staring at them. "Don Luis? Alive? I thought— Arrest? What for?"

Elia's embarrassment was painful to see. Luz answered, "For killing Herman Macmilan."

Vera stared; the pulse of her heart throbbed in her swollen temple.

"I didn't see it," Luz said in her dry calm voice. "I was back in the crowd with Southwind. Andre was up front with Lev and Elia, he saw it and told me. It was after Macmilan shot Lev. Before any of us knew what was happening. Macmilan's men were just beginning to shoot at us. My father took a gun out of one of the men's hands and used it like a club. He didn't shoot it, Andre said. I suppose it was hard to tell, after the fighting there, and people trampling back and forth over them, but Andre said they thought the blow must have killed Macmilan. Anyway he was dead when they came back."

"I saw it too," Elia said, thickly. "It was— I suppose it was what—what kept some of the City men from shooting, they were confused—"

"No order was ever given," Luz said. "So there was time for the marchers to rush in on them. Andre thinks that if my father hadn't turned on Macmilan, there would have been no fighting at all. Just them shooting and the marchers running."

"And no betrayal of our principles," said Southwind, clearly and steadily. "Perhaps, if we hadn't rushed forward, the City men wouldn't have fired in self-defense."

"And only Lev would have been killed?" Luz said, equally clearly. "But Macmilan would have ordered them all to fire, Southwind. He'd started it. If the marchers had run away sooner, yes, maybe fewer would have been shot. And no City men beaten to death. Your principles would be all right. But Lev would still be dead. And Macmilan would be alive."

Elia was looking at her with an expression she had not seen before; she did not know what it meant—detestation, perhaps, or fear.

"Why," Vera said in a pitiful dry whisper.

"I don't know!" Luz said, and because it was such a relief to be saying these things, talking about them, instead of hiding them and saying everything was all right, she actually laughed. "Do I understand what my father does, what he thinks, what he is? Maybe he went insane. That's what old Marquez told Andre, last week. I know if I'd been where he was, I would have killed Macmilan too. But that doesn't explain why *he* did it. There is no explanation. It's easiest to say he was insane. You see, that's what's wrong with your ideas, Southwind, you people. They're all true, all right and true, violence gains nothing, killing wins nothing—only sometimes nothing is what people want. Death is what they want. And they get it."

There was a silence.

"Councillor Falco saw the folly of Macmilan's act," Elia said. "He was trying to prevent—"

"No," Luz said, "he wasn't. He wasn't trying to prevent more shooting, more killing, and he wasn't on your side. Don't you have anything in your head but reason, Senhor Elia? My father killed Macmilan for the same 'reason' that Lev stood up there facing the men with guns and defying them and got killed. Because he was a man, that's what men do. The reasons come afterward."

Elia's hands were clenched; his face was pale, so that his blue eyes stood out unnaturally bright. He looked straight at Luz and said, gently enough, "Why do you stay here, Luz Marina?"

"Where else should I go?" she asked, almost jeering.

"To your father."

"Yes, that's what women do. . . ."

"He is in distress, in disgrace; he needs you."

"And you don't."

"Yes, we do," Vera said, with desperation. "Elia, are you insane too? Are you trying to drive her out?"

"It was because of her— If she hadn't come here, Lev— It was her fault—" Elia was in the grip of emotion he could not master, his voice going high, his eyes wide. "It was her fault!"

"What are you saying?" Vera whispered, and Southwind, fiercely, "It was not! None of it!"

Luz said nothing.

Elia, shaking, put his hands over his face. No one said anything for a long time.

"I'm sorry," he said, looking up. His eyes were dry and bright, his mouth worked strangely as he spoke.

"Forgive me, Luz Marina. There was no meaning in what I said. You came to us, you're welcome here among us. I get—I get very tired, trying to see what ought to be done, what's right—it's hard to see what's right—"

The three women were silent.

"I compromise, yes, I compromise with Marquez, what else can I do? Then you say, Elia is betraying our ideals, selling us into permanent bondage to the City, losing all we struggled for. What do you want, then? More deaths? You want another confrontation, you want to see the People of the Peace being shot again, fighting, beating—beating men to death again —we who—who believe in peace, in nonviolence—"

"Nobody is saying that of you, Elia," Vera said.

"We have to go slowly. We must be reasonable. We can't do it all at once, rashly, violently. It's not easy—not easy!"

"No," Vera said. "It's not easy."

"We came from all over the world," the old man said. "From great cities and from little villages, the people came. When the March began in the City of Moskva there were four thousand, and when they reached the edge of the place called Russia already there were seven thousand. And they walked across the great place called Europe, and always hundreds and hundreds of people joined the March, families and single souls, young and old. They came from towns nearby, they came from great lands far away over the oceans, India, Africa. They all brought what they could bring of food and precious money to buy

food, for so many marchers always needed food. The
people of the towns stood along the side of the road
to watch the marchers pass, and sometimes children
ran out with presents of food or precious money.
The armies of the great countries stood along the
roadside too, and watched, and protected the
marchers, and made sure they did no damage to the
fields and trees and towns, by being so many. And
the marchers sang, and sometimes the armies sang
with them, and sometimes the men of the armies
threw away their guns and joined the March in the
darkness of the night. They walked, they walked. At
night they camped and it was like a great town growing up all at once in the open fields, all the people.
They walked, they walked, they walked, across the
fields of France and across the fields of Germany and
across the high mountains of Spain, weeks they walked
and months they walked, singing the songs of peace,
and so they came at last, ten thousand strong, to the
end of the land and the beginning of the sea, to the
City Lisboa, where the ships had been promised
them. And there the ships lay in harbor.

"So that was the Long March. But it wasn't over,
the journey! They went into the ships, to sail to the
Free Land, where they would be welcomed. But there
were too many of them now. The ships would hold
only two thousand, and their numbers had grown
and grown as they marched, there were ten thousand
of them now. What were they to do? They crowded,
they crowded; they built more beds, they crowded
ten to a room of the great ships, a room that was

meant to hold two. The ships' masters said, Stop, you can't crowd the ships any more, there isn't enough water for the long voyage, you can't all come aboard the ships. So they bought boats, fishing boats, boats with sails and with engines; and people, grand rich people, with boats of their own, came and said, Use my boat, I'll take fifty souls to the Free Land. Fishermen came from the city called England and said, Use my boat, I'll take fifty souls. Some were afraid of the small boats, to cross so great a sea; some went back home then, and left the Long March. But always new people came to join them, so their numbers grew. And so at last they all sailed from the harbor of Lisboa, and music played and there were ribbons in the wind and all the people in the great ships and the little boats sailed out together singing.

"They couldn't stay together on the sea. The ships were fast, the boats were slow. In eight days the big ships sailed into the harbor of Montral, in the land of Canamerica. The other boats came after, strung out all across the ocean, some days behind, some weeks behind. My parents were on one of the boats, a beautiful white boat named *Anita*, that a noble lady had lent to the People of the Peace so that they could come to the Free Land. There were forty on that boat. Those were good days, my mother said. The weather was good and they sat on the deck in the sun and planned how they would build the City of Peace in the land they had been promised, the land between the mountains, in the northern part of Canamerica.

"But when they came to Montral, they were met by

men with guns, and taken, and put into prisons; and
there were all the others, from the big ships, all the
people, waiting, in the prison camps.

"There were too many of them, the leaders of that
land said. There were to have been two thousand,
and there were ten thousand. There was no land or
place for so many. They were dangerous, being so
many. People from all over the Earth kept coming
there to join them, and camping outside the city
and outside the prison camps, and singing the songs
of peace. Even from Brasil they were coming, they
had begun their own Long March northward up the
length of the great continents. The rulers of Canamerica were frightened. They said there was no way
to keep order, or to feed so many. They said this was
an invasion. They said the Peace was a lie, not the
truth, because they didn't understand it and didn't
want it. They said their own people were leaving them
and joining the Peace, and this could not be allowed,
because they must all fight the Long War with the
Republic, that had been fought for twenty years and
still was being fought. They said the People of the
Peace were traitors, and spies from the Republic! And
so they put us into the prison camps, instead of giving
that land between the mountains they had promised
us. There I was born, in the prison camp of Montral.

"At last the rulers said: Very well, we'll keep our
promise, we'll give you land to live on, but there's
no place for you on Earth. We'll give you the ship
that was built in Brasil long ago, to send thieves and
murderers away. Three ships they built, two they

sent out to the world called Victoria, the third they
never used because their law was changed. No one
wants the ship because it was made to make only the
one voyage, it cannot come back to Earth. Brasil has
given us that ship. Two thousand of you are to go in
it, that is all it can hold. And the rest of you must
either find your way back to your own land across the
ocean, back to Russia the Black, or live here in the
prison camps making weapons for the War with the
Republic. All your leaders must go on the ship,
Mehta and Adelson, Kaminskaya and Wicewska and
Shults; we will not have those men and women on
the Earth, because they do not love the War. They
must take the Peace to another world.

"So the two thousand were chosen by lot. And the
choosing was bitter, the bitterest day of all the bitter
days. For those that went, there was hope, but at
what risk—going out unpiloted across the stars to an
unknown world, never to return? And for those that
must stay, there was no hope left. For there was no
place left for the Peace on Earth.

"So the choice was made, and the tears were wept,
and the ship was sent. And so, for those two thousand,
and for their children and the children of their children, the Long March has ended. Here in the place we
named Shantih, in the valleys of Victoria. But we do
not forget the Long March and the great voyage and
those we left behind, their arms stretched out to us.
We do not forget the Earth."

The children listened: fair faces and dark, black
hair and brown; eyes intent, drowsy; enjoying the
story, moved by it, bored by it. . . . They had all

heard it before, young as some of them were. It was
part of the world to them. Only to Luz was it new.

There were a hundred questions in her mind, too
many; she let the children ask their questions. "Is
Amity black because her grandmother came from
Russia the Black?"—"Tell about the space ship! about
how they went to sleep on the space ship!"—"Tell
about the animals on Earth!"— Some of the questions were asked for her; they wanted her, the outsider, the big girl who didn't know, to hear their
favorite parts of the saga of their people. "Tell Luz
about the flying-air-planes!" cried a little girl, very
excited, and turning to Luz began to gabble the old
man's story for him: "His mother and father were on
the boat in the middle of the sea and a flying ship
went over them in the air, and went boom and fell
in the sea and blew up and that was the Republic, and
they saw it. And they tried to pick people up out of
the water but there weren't any and the water was
poisonous and they had to go on."—"Tell about the
people that came from Afferca!" a boy demanded.
But Hari was tired. "Enough now," he said. "Let's
sing one of the songs of the Long March. Meria?"

A girl of twelve stood up, smiling, and faced the
others. "O when we come," she began in a sweet
ringing voice, and the others joined in—

> O when we come,
> O when we come to Lisboa,
> The white ships will be waiting
> O when we come. . . .

* * *

The clouds were moving away, heavy and ragged-fringed, over the river and the northern hills. To the south a streak of the outer Bay lay silver and remote. Drops from the last rainfall fell heavy now and then from the leaves of the big cottonwool trees on the summit of this hill that stood east of Southwind's house; there was no other sound. A silent world, a gray world. Luz stood alone under the trees, looking out over the empty land. She had not been alone for a long time. She had not known, when she set off toward the hill, where she was going, what she was looking for. This place, this silence, this solitude. Her feet had borne her toward herself.

The ground was muddy, the weeds heavy with wet, but the poncho-coat Italia had given her was thick; she sat down on the springy leaf mold under the trees, and with arms around knees beneath the poncho sat still, gazing westward over the bend of the river. She sat so for a long time, seeing nothing but the moveless land, the slow-moving clouds and river.

Alone, alone. She was alone. She had not had time to know that she was alone, working with Southwind, nursing Vera, talking with Andre, joining little by little in the life of Shantih; helping to set up the new Town school, for the City school was closed henceforth to the people of Shantih; drawn in as guest to this house and that, this family and that; drawn in, made welcome, for they were gentle people, inexpert in resentment or distrust. Only at night, on the straw mattress in the dark of the loft, had it come to her, her loneliness, wearing a white and bitter face. She had been frightened, then. What shall I do? she had cried in her mind, and turning over to escape the bitter face of her solitude, had taken refuge in her weariness, in sleep.

It came to her now, walking softly along the gray hilltop. Its face now was Lev's face. She had no wish to turn away.

It was time to look at what she had lost. To look at it and see it all. The sunset of spring over the roofs of the City, long ago, and his face lit by that glory— "There, there, you can see what it should be, what it is. . . ." The dusk of the room in Southwind's house, and his face, his eyes. "To live and die for the sake of the spirit—" The wind and light on Rocktop Hill, and his voice. And the rest, all the rest, all the days and lights and winds and years that would have been, and that would not be, that should be and were not, because he was dead. Shot dead on the road, in the wind, at twenty-one. His mountains unclimbed, never to be climbed.

If the spirit stayed in the world, Luz thought, that was where it had gone, by now: north to the valley he had found, to the mountains he had told her of, the last night before the march on the City, with such joy and yearning: "Higher than you can imagine, Luz, higher and whiter. You look up, and then up, and still there are peaks above the peaks."

He would be there, now, not here. It was only her own solitude she looked at, though it wore his face.

"Go on, Læv," she whispered aloud. "Go on to the mountains, go higher. . . ."

But where shall I go? Where shall I go, alone?

Without Lev, without the mother I never knew and the father I can never know, without my house and my City, without a friend—oh, yes, friends, Vera, Southwind, Andre, all the others, all the gentle people, but they're not my people. Only Lev, only Lev was, and he couldn't stay, he wouldn't wait, he had to go climb his mountain, and put life off till later. He was my chance, my luck. And I was his. But he wouldn't see it, he wouldn't stop and look. He threw it all away.

So now I stop here, between the valleys, under the trees, and I have to look. And what I see is Lev dead, and his hope lost; my father a murderer and mad; and I a traitor to the City and a stranger in the Town.

And what else is there?

All the rest of the world. The river there, and the hills, and the light on the Bay. All the rest of this silent living world, with no people in it. And I alone.

As she came down from the hill she saw Andre coming out of Southwind's house, turning to speak to Vera at the door. They called to each other across the fallow fields, and he waited for her at the turn of the lane that led to Shantih.

"Where were you, Luz?" he asked in his concerned, shy way. He never, like the others, tried to draw her in; he was simply there, reliable. Since Lev's death there had been no joy for him, and much anxiety. He stood there now, sturdy and a little stooped, over-burdened, patient.

"Nowhere," she answered, truthfully. "Just walking. Thinking. Andre, tell me. I never want to ask you while Vera's there, I don't like to upset her. What will happen now, between the City and Shantih? I don't know enough to understand what Elia says. Will it just go on the way it was—before?"

After a fairly long pause, Andre nodded. His dark face, with jutting cheekbones like carved wood, was shut tight. "Or worse," he said. Then, scrupulous to be fair to Elia, "Some things are better. The trade agreement—if they keep to it. And the South Valley expansion. There won't be forced labor, or 'estates' and all that. I'm hopeful about that. We may work together there, for once."

"Will you go there?"

"I don't know. I suppose so. I should."

"What about the northern colony? The valley you found, the mountains?"

Andre looked up at her. He shook his head.

"No way—?"

"Only if we went as their servants."

"Marquez won't agree to your going alone, without City people?"

He shook his head.

"What if you went anyway?"

"What do you think I dream of every night?" he said, and for the first time there was bitterness in his voice. "After I've been with Elia and Jewel and Sam and Marquez and the Council, talking compromise, talking cooperation, talking reason?—But if we went, they'd follow."

"Then go where they can't follow."

"Where would that be?" Andre said, his voice patient again, ironic and miserable.

"Anywhere! Farther east, into the forests. Or southeast. Or south, down the coast, down past where the trawlers go—there must be other bays, other town sites! This is a whole continent, a whole world. Why do we have to stay here, here, huddled up here, destroying each other? You've been in the wilderness, you and Lev and the others, you know what it's like—"

"Yes. I do."

"You came back. Why must you come back? Why couldn't people just go, not too many of them all at once, but just go, at night, and go on; maybe a few should go ahead and make stopping-places with supplies; but you don't leave a trail, any trail. You just go. Far! And when you've gone a hundred kilometers, or five hundred, or a thousand, and you find a good place, you stop, and make a settlement. A new place. Alone."

"It's not—it breaks the community, Luz," Andre said. "It would be . . . running away."

"Oh," Luz said, and her eyes shone with anger. "Running away! You crawl into Marquez's trap in the South Valley and call that standing firm! You talk about choice and freedom— The world, the whole world is there for you to live in and be free, and that would be running away! From what? To what? Maybe we can't be free, maybe people always take themselves with themselves, but at least you can try. What was your Long March for? What makes you think it ever ended?"

11

Vera had meant to stay awake to see them off, but she had fallen asleep by the fire, and the soft knock at the door did not waken her. Southwind and Luz looked at each other; Southwind shook her head. Luz knelt and hastily, as silently as she could, laid a fresh square of peat behind the coals, so the house would stay warm through the night. Southwind, made awkward by her heavy coat and backpack, stooped and touched Vera's gray hair with her lips; then she looked around the house, a bewildered, hurried look, and went out. Luz followed her.

The night was cloudy but dry, very dark. The cold of it woke Luz from her long trance of waiting, and she caught her breath. There were people around her in the dark, a few soft voices. "Both there? All right, come on." They set off, past the house, through the potato field, toward the low ridge that lay behind it to the east. As Luz's eyes became accustomed to the dark she made out that the person who walked beside her was Lev's father, Sasha; sensing her gaze in the darkness he said, "How's the pack?"

"It's all right," she said in a bare whisper. They must not talk, they must not make any noise, she thought, not yet, not till they were clear of the settlement, past the last village and the last farm, across

Mill River, a long way. They must go fast and silently, and not be stopped, O Lord God please not be stopped!

"Mine's made of iron ingots, or unforgiven sins," Sasha murmured; and they went on in silence, a dozen shadows in the shadow of the world.

It was still dark when they came to Mill River, a few kilometers south of where it joined the Songe. The boat was waiting, Andre and Holdfast waiting with it. Hari rowed six across, then the second six. Luz was in the second lot. As they neared the eastern shore the solid blackness of the nightworld was growing insubstantial, a veil of light dimming all things, a mist thickening on the water. Shivering, she set foot on the far shore. Left alone in the boat, which Andre and the others had already pushed off again, Hari called out softly, "Good luck, good luck! Peace go with you!" And the boat vanished into the mist like a ghost; and the twelve stood there on the ghostly, fading sand.

"Up this way," said Andre's voice out of the mist and pallor. "They'll have breakfast for us."

They were the last and smallest of the three groups to leave, one group a night; the others were waiting farther on among the rugged hills east of the Mill, country where only coney trappers went. In single file, following Andre and Holdfast, they left the river-bank and set off into the wild land.

She had been thinking for hours and hours, step after step, that as soon as they stopped she would sink right down on the dirt or the mud or the sand, sink down and not move again till morning. But when they stopped she saw Martin and Andre, up at the front, discussing something, and she went on, step after step, till she came up with them, and even then did not sink down, but kept standing, to hear what they were talking about.

"Martin thinks the compass isn't reading true," Andre said. With a dubious look, he held the instrument out to Luz, as if she could judge its inaccuracy at a glance. What she saw was its delicacy, the box of polished wood, the gold ring, the glass, the frail burnished needle hovering, trembling between the finely incised points: what a beautiful thing, miraculous, improbable, she thought. But Martin was looking at it with disapproval. "I'm sure it's pulling east," he said. "Must be iron-ore masses in those hills, deflecting it." He nodded toward the east. For a day and a half they had been in a queer scrubby country that bore no ringtrees or cottonwools but only a sparse, tangled scrub which grew no more than a couple of meters high; it was not forest, but not open country; there was seldom any long view. But they knew that to the east, to their left, the line of high hills they had first seen six days ago went on. Whenever they came up on a rise in the scrublands, they saw the dark red, rocky skyline of the heights.

"Well," Luz said, hearing her own voice for the first time in hours, "does it matter much?"

Andre chewed his lower lip. His face looked bone weary, the eyes narrowed and lifeless. "Not for going on," he said. "So long as we have the sun or some stars at night. But for making the map. . . ."

"What if we turn east again. Get over those hills. They aren't getting any lower," Martin said. A younger man than Andre, he looked far less tired. He was one of the mainstays of the group. Luz felt at ease with Martin; he looked like a City man, stocky, dark, well muscled, rather curt and somber; even his name was a common one in the City. But for all Martin's comfortable strength, it was to Andre that she turned with her question.

"Can't we mark the trail yet?"

Unwilling to make any trail that could be followed, they had tried to map their course. A map could be brought back to Shantih by a few messengers, after a couple of years, to guide a second group to the new colony. That was the only reason for making it that they ever spoke of. Andre, the map maker of the northern journey, was in charge of it, and he felt his responsibility as a heavy one, for the unspoken purpose of the map was always in their minds. It was their one link to Shantih, to humankind, to their own past lives; their one assurance that they were not simply wandering lost in the wilderness, aimless, without goal and, since they could mark no trail, without hope of return.

At times Luz clung to the idea of the map, at times she was impatient with it. Martin was keen on it, but his keenest care was that they keep their trail covered; he winced, Italia remarked, when anybody stepped on a stick and broke it. Certainly they had left, in the ten days of their journey, as little mark of their going as sixty-seven people could leave.

Martin was shaking his head at Luz's question.

"Look," he said, "our choice of route has been so obvious, the easiest way, right from the start."

Andre smiled. It was a dry crack of a smile, like a crack in tree bark, and narrowed his eyes to two lesser cracks. That was why Luz liked to be with Andre, drew strength from him, that humorous patient smile, like a tree smiling.

"Consider the options, Martin!" he said, and she saw what he was imagining: a party of City men, Macmilan's bullies, guns and whips and boots and all, standing on the bluffs of the Songe, looking north, east, south, over the gray rusty-ringed rising falling rain-darkened unending trackless voiceless enormous wilderness, and trying to decide which, of a hundred possible directions, the fugitives had chosen.

"All right," she said, "let's cross the hills, then."

"Climbing won't be much harder than slogging through this scrub," Andre said.

Martin nodded. "Turn east again here, then?"

"Here as well as anywhere," said Andre, and got out his grubby, dog-eared sketch map to make a note.

"Now?" Luz asked. "Or camp?"

They usually did not camp till near sundown, but they had come a long way today. She looked around the shoulder-high, thorny, bronze-colored bushes, which grew spaced a meter or two apart so that millions of pointless winding trails led around and between and amongst them. Only a few of the group were visible; most of them had sat right down to rest when the halt was called. Overhead was a lead-gray sky, featureless, one even cloud. No rain had fallen for two nights, but the weather was getting colder every hour.

"Well, a few more kilos," Andre said, "and we'd be at the foot of the hills; might find some shelter there. And water." He looked at her judgingly, and waited for her judgment. He, Martin, Italia, the other path-finders, often used her and a couple of the older women as representatives of the weak, the ones who could not keep the pace the strongest would have kept. She did not mind. She walked each day right to the limit of her endurance, or beyond it. The first three days of the journey, when they had been hurry-ing, afraid of pursuit, had exhausted her, and though she was growing tougher she never could make up that initial loss. She accepted this, and saved all her resentment for her backpack, that monstrous and irascible, knee-bending, neck-destroying load. If only they didn't have to carry everything with them! But they could not push carts without making, or leaving, paths; and sixty-seven people could not live off the wilderness while traveling, or settle in it without tools, even if it were not late autumn getting on to winter. . . .

"A few more kilos," she said. She was always sur-prised when she said things like that. "A few more kilos," as if it were nothing at all, when for the last six hours she had longed, craved to sit down, just to sit down, just to sit down for a minute, a month, a year! But now they had spoken of turning east again she found she also craved to get out of this dreary maze of thorn-scrub, into the hills, where maybe you could see your way ahead.

"Few minutes' rest," she added, and, sat down, slipping off her pack straps and rubbing her aching shoulders. Andre promptly sat down too. Martin went off to talk with some of the others and discuss the change of course. None of them was visible, they had all vanished in the sea of thorn-scrub, taking their few minutes' rest already, flat out on the sandy, grayish soil littered with thorns. She could not see even Andre, only a corner of his pack. A northwest wind, faint but cold, rustled the little dry branches of the bushes. There was no other sound.

Sixty-seven people: no sight of them, no sound of them. Vanished. Lost. A drop of water in the river, a word blown off on the wind. Some small creatures moved a little while in the wilderness, not going very far, and then ceased to move, and it made no difference to the wilderness, or to anything, no more difference than the dropping of one thorn among a million thorns or the shifting of a grain of sand.

The fear she had come to know these ten days of their journeying came up like a small gray fog in the fields of her mind, a chill creep of blindness. It was hers, hers by inheritance and training; it was to keep out her fear, their fear, that the roofs and walls of the City had been raised; it was fear that had drawn the streets so straight, and made the doors so narrow. She had scarcely known it, living behind those doors. She had felt quite safe. Even in Shantih she had forgotten it, stranger as she was, for the walls there were not visible but were very strong: companionship, cooperation, love; the close human circle. But she had walked away from that, by choice, and walked out into the wilderness, and come face to face at last with the fear that all her life had been built upon.

She could not simply face it, but had to fight it when it first began to come upon her, or it would blot out everything, and she would lose the power of choice entirely. She had to fight blindly, for no reason stood against that fear. It was a great deal older and stronger than ideas.

There was the idea of God. Back in the City they talked about God to children. He made all the worlds, and he punished the wicked, and sent good people up to Heaven when they died. Heaven was a beautiful house with a gold roof where Meria, God's mother, everybody's mother, tenderly waited for the souls of the dead. She had liked that story. When she was little she had prayed to God to make things happen and not happen, because he could do anything if you asked him; later she had liked to imagine God's mother and her mother keeping house together. But when she thought of Heaven here, it was small and far away, like the City. It had nothing to do with the wilderness. There was no God here; he belonged to people, and where there were no people there was no God. At the funeral for Lev and the others they had talked about God, too, but that was back there, back there. Here there was nothing like that. Nobody had made this wilderness, and there was no evil in it and no good; it simply was.

She drew a circle in the sandy dirt near her foot, making it as perfect as she could, using a thorny twig to draw it with. That was a world, or a self, or God, that circle, you could call it anything. Nothing else in the wilderness could think of a circle like that —she thought of the delicate gold ring around the compass glass. Because she was human, she had the mind and eyes and skillful hand to imagine the idea of a circle and to draw the idea. But any drop of water falling from a leaf into a pool or rain puddle could make a circle, a more perfect one, fleeting outward from the center, and if there were no boundary to the water the circle would fleet outward forever, fainter and fainter, forever larger. She could not do that, which any drop of water could do. Inside her circle what was there? Grains of sand, dust, a few tiny pebbles, a half-buried thorn, Andre's tired face, the sound of Southwind's voice, Sasha's eyes which were like Lev's eyes, the ache of her own shoulders where the pack straps pulled, and her fear. The circle could not keep out the fear. And the hand erased the circle, smoothing out the sand, leaving it as it had always been and would always be after they had gone on.

"At first I felt that I was leaving Timmo behind," Southwind said, as she studied the worst blister on her left foot. "When we left the house. He and I built it . . . you know. I felt as if I was walking away and finally leaving him forever, leaving him behind. But now it doesn't seem that way. It was out here he died, in the wilderness. Not here, I know; way back up north there. But I don't feel that he's so terribly far away as I did all autumn living in our house, it's almost as if I'd come out to join him. Not dying, I don't mean that. It's just that there I only thought about his death, and here, while we're walking, all the time, I think about him alive. As if he was with me now."

They had camped in a fold of the land just under the red hills, beside a lively, rocky stream. They had built their fires, cooked, and eaten; many were already stretched out in their blankets to sleep. It was not dark yet, but so cold that if you weren't moving about you must either huddle to the fire or wrap up and sleep. The first five nights of the journey they had not built fires, for fear of pursuers, and those had been miserable nights; Luz had never known such a pure delight as she had felt at their first campfire, back in a great tree-ring on the south slope of the badlands, and every night that pleasure came again, the utter luxury of hot food, of warmth. The three families she and Southwind camped and cooked with were settling down for the night; the youngest child—the youngest of the whole migration, a boy of eleven—was curled up like a pouchbat in his blanket already, fast asleep. Luz tended the fire, while Southwind tended her blisters. Up and down the riverbank were seven other fires, the farthest no more than a candle flame in the blue-gray dusk, a spot of hazy, trembling gold. The noise of the stream covered any sound of voices round the other fires.

"I'll get some more brushwood," Luz said. She was not avoiding an answer to what Southwind had said. No answer was needed. Southwind was gentle and complete; she gave and spoke, expecting no return; in all the world there could be no companion less demanding, or more encouraging.

They had done a good day's walk, twenty-seven kilometers by Martin's estimate; they had got out of that drab nightmare labyrinth of scrub; they had had a hot dinner, the fire was hot, and it was not raining. Even the ache in Luz's shoulders was pleasant (because the pack was not pulling on them) when she stood up. It was these times at the day's end, by the fire, that counterweighed the long dreary hungry afternoons of walking and walking and walking and trying to ease the cut of the pack straps on her shoulders, and the hours in the mud and rain when there seemed to be no reason at all to go on, and the worst hours, in the black dark of the night, when she woke always from the same terrible dream: that there was a circle of some things, not people, standing around their camp, just out of sight, not visible in the darkness, but watching.

"This one's better," Southwind said when Luz came back with an armload of wood from the thickets up the slope, "but the one on my heel isn't. You know, all today I've been feeling that we aren't being followed."

"I don't think we ever were," Luz said, building up the fire. "I never did think they'd really care, even if they knew. They don't want to think about the wilderness, in the City. They want to pretend it isn't there."

"I hope so. I hated feeling that we were running. Being explorers is a much braver feeling."

Luz got the fire settled to burning low but warm, and squatted by it simply soaking the heat up for some while.

"I miss Vera," she said. Her throat was dry with the dust of walking, and she did not use her voice often these days; it sounded dry and harsh to her, like her father's voice.

"She'll come with the second group," Southwind said with comfortable certainty, winding a cloth strip around her pretty, battered foot, and tying it off firmly at the ankle. "Ah, that feels better. I'm going to wrap my feet tomorrow like Holdfast does. It'll be warmer, too."

"If it just won't rain."

"It won't rain tonight." The Shantih people were much weather-wiser than Luz. They had not lived so much within doors as she, they knew what the wind meant, even here, where the winds were different.

"It might tomorrow," Southwind added, beginning to wriggle into her blanket-bag, her voice already sounding small and warm.

"Tomorrow we'll be up in the hills," Luz said. She looked up, to the east, but the near slope of the stream valley and the blue-gray dusk hid that rocky skyline. The clouds had thinned; a star shone out for a while high in the east, small and misty, then vanished as the unseen clouds rejoined. Luz watched for it to reappear, but it did not. She felt foolishly disappointed. The sky was dark now, the ground was dark. No light anywhere, except the eight gold flecks, their campfires, a tiny constellation in the night. And far off there, days behind them in the west, thousands and thousands of steps behind them, behind the scrubland and the badland and the hills and the valleys and the streams, beside the great river running to the sea, a few more lights: the City and the Town, a tiny huddle of yellow-lit windows. The river dark, running in darkness. And no light on the sea.

She reset a log to smolder more slowly, and banked the ashes against it. She found her sleeping bag and wriggled down into it, next to Southwind. She wanted to talk, now. Southwind had seldom spoken much of Timmo. She wanted to hear her talk about him, and about Lev; she wanted for the first time to speak about Lev herself. There was too much silence here. Things would get lost in the silence. One should speak. And Southwind would understand. She too had lost her luck, and known death, and gone on.

Luz said her name softly, but the warm blanket-bundle next to her did not stir. Southwind was asleep.

Luz settled down cautiously, getting herself comfortable. The river beach, though stony, was a better bed than last night's in the thorny scrubland. But her body was so tired that it felt heavy, unwieldy, hard; her chest was hard and tight. She closed her eyes. At once she saw the hall of Casa Falco, long and serene, the silver light reflected from the Bay filling the windows; and her father standing there, erect, alert, self-contained, as he always stood. But he was standing there doing nothing, which was not like him. Michael and Teresa were off in the doorway, whispering together. She felt a curious resentment toward them. Her father stood with his back to them, as if he did not know they were there, or as if he knew it, but was afraid of them. He raised his arms in a strange way. She saw his face for a moment. He was crying. She could not breathe, she tried to draw a long breath but could not; it caught; because she was crying—deep shaking sobs from which she could scarcely gasp a breath before the next came. Racked with sobs, lying shaken and tormented on the ground in the enormous night, she wept for the dead, for the lost. Not fear now, but grief, the grief past enduring, that endures.

Her weariness and the darkness drank her tears, and she fell asleep before she was done weeping. She slept all night without dreams or evil wakings, like a stone among the stones.

The hills were high and hard. The uphill going was not bad, for they could zigzag up across the great, open, rusty slopes, but when they got to the top, among the rimrock piled like houses and towers, they saw that they had climbed only the first of a triple or quadruple chain of hills, and that the farther ridges were higher.

In the canyons between the ridges ringtrees crowded, not growing in rings but jammed close and shooting up unnaturally high toward the light. The heavy shrub called aloes crowded between the red trunks, making the going very difficult; but there was still fruit on the aloes, thick rich dark flesh wrinkled about a center seed, a welcome addition to the scanty food in their packs. In this country they had no choice but to leave a trail behind them: they had to cut their way with brush hooks to get on at all. They were a day getting through the canyon, another climbing the second line of hills, beyond which lay the next chain of canyons massed with bronze trees and crimson underbrush, and beyond it a formidable ridge, steep-spurred, rising in bare screes to the rock-capped summit.

They had to camp down in the gorge the next night. Even Martin, after cutting and hacking their way forward step by step, by mid-afternoon was too tired to go on. When they camped, those who were not worn out from path-making spread out from the camp, cautiously and not going far, for in the undergrowth you could lose all sense of direction very easily. They found and picked aloes, and several of the boys, led by Welcome, found freshwater mussels in the stream at the bottom of the gorge when they went for water. They had a good meal that night. They needed it, for it was raining again. Mist, rain, evening grayed the heavy vivid reds of the forest. They built up brushwood shelters and huddled by fires which would not stay alight.

"I saw a queer thing, Luz."

He was a strange fellow, Sasha; the oldest of them all, though tough and wiry, better able to keep up than some of the younger men; never out of temper, totally self-reliant, and almost totally silent. Luz had never seen him take part in a conversation beyond a yes or no, a smile or head shake. She knew he had never spoken at the Meeting House, never been one of Elia's group or Vera's people, never been a choice-maker among his people, though he was the son of one of their great heroes and leaders, Shults who had led the Long March from the streets of the City Moskva to the Port of Lisboa, and on. Shults had had other children, but they had died in the first hard years on Victoria; only Sasha, last-born, Victoria-born, had lived. And had fathered a son, and seen him die. He never talked. Only, sometimes, to her, to Luz. "I saw a queer thing, Luz."

"What?"

"An animal." He pointed to the right, up the steep slope of brush and trees, a dark wall now in the fading light. "There's a bit of a clearing up there where a couple of big trees went down and cleared some room. Found some aloes at one end of it and was picking them. Looked over my shoulder—felt something watching. It was at the far end of the clearing." He paused a minute, not for effect but to order his description. "It was gathering aloes too. I thought it was a man at first. Like a man. But it wasn't much bigger than a coney, when it went down on all fours. Dark-colored, with a reddish head—a big head, seemed too big for the rest of it. A center eye, like a wotsit, looking at me. Eyes on the sides too, I think, but I couldn't see it clear enough. It stared a minute and then it turned and went into the trees."

His voice was low and even.

"It sounds frightening," Luz said quietly, "I don't know why." But she did know why, thinking of her dream of the beings who came and watched; though she had not had the dream since they were in the scrublands.

Sasha shook his head. They were squatting side by side under a rough roof of branches. He rubbed the beaded rain off his hair, rubbed down his bristling gray mustache. "There's nothing here will hurt us," he said. "Except ourselves. Are there any stories in the City about animals we don't know of?"

"No—only the scures."

"Scures?"

"Old stories. Creatures like men, with glaring eyes, hairy. My cousin Lores talked about them. My father said they *were* men—exiles, or men who had wandered off, crazy men, gone wild."

Sasha nodded. "Nothing like that would come this far," he said. "We're the first."

"We've only lived there on the coast. I suppose there are animals we've never seen before."

"Plants too. See that, it's like what we call white-berry, but it's not the same. I never saw it until yesterday."

Presently he said, "There's no name for the animal I saw."

Luz nodded.

Between her and Sasha was silence, the bond of silence. He did not speak of the animal to others, nor did she. They knew nothing of this world, their world, only that they must walk in it in silence, until they had learned a language fitting to be spoken here. He was one who was willing to wait.

The second ridge climbed, in a third day of rain. A longer, shallower valley, where the going was easier. About midday the wind turned, blowing down from the north, scouring the ridges free of cloud and mist. All afternoon they climbed the last slope, and that evening in a vast, cold clarity of light they came up among the massive, rusty rock-formations of the summit, and saw the eastern lands.

They gathered there slowly, the slowest still struggling up the stony slope while the leaders stood waiting for them—a few tiny dark figures, to the climbers' eyes, against an immense bright emptiness of sky. The short, sparse grass of the ridge top glowed ruddy in the sunset. They all gathered there, sixty-seven people, and stood looking out over the rest of the world. They said little. The rest of the world looked very large.

The shadows of the ridge they had been climbing stretched a long way across the plain. Beyond those shadows the land was gold, a hazy, reddish, wintry gold, dimly streaked and mottled with courses of distant streams and the bulk of low hills or ringtree groves. Far across that plateau, at the very edge of the eyes' reach, mountains rose against the tremendous, colorless, windy sky.

"How far?" someone asked.

"A hundred kilometers to the foothills, maybe."

"They're big. . . ."

"Like the ones we saw in the north, over Lake Serene."

"It may be the same range. It ran southeastward."

"That plain is like the sea, it goes on and on."

"It's cold up here!"

"Let's get down over the summit, out of the wind."

Long after the high plains had sunk into gray, the keen small edge of sunlit ice burned there at the edge of vision in the east. It whitened and faded; the stars came out, thick in the windy blackness, all the constellations, all the bright cities that were not their home.

Wild bog-rice grew thick by the streams of the plateau; they lived on that during the eight days of their crossing. The Iron Hills shrank behind them, a wrinkled rusty line drawn down the west. The plain was alive with coneys, a longer-legged breed than those of the coastal forests; the riverbanks were pocked and hollowed with their warrens, and when the sun was out the coneys came out, and sat in the sun, and watched the people pass with tranquil, uninterested eyes.

"You'd have to be a fool to starve here," Holdfast said, watching Italia lay her snares near a glittering, stony ford.

But they went on. The wind blew bitter on that high, open land, and there was no wood to build with, or to burn. They went on until the land began to swell, rising toward the foothills of the mountains, and they came to a big river, south-running, which Andre the map maker named the Grayrock. To cross it they must find a ford, which looked unlikely, or build rafts. Some were for crossing, putting that barrier too behind them. Others were for turning south again and going on along the west bank of the river. While they deliberated, they set up their first stopping-place camp. One of the men had hurt his foot in a fall, and there were several other minor injuries and troubles; their footgear needed mending; they were all weary, and needed a few days' rest. They put up shelters of brushwood and thatchleaf, the first day. It was cold, with gathering clouds, though the bitter wind did not blow here. That night the first snow fell.

It seldom snowed at Songe Bay; never this early in the winter. They were no longer in the soft climate of the western coast. The coastal hills, the badlands, and the Iron Hills caught the rain that came in on the west winds off the sea; here it would be dryer, but colder.

The great range toward which they had been walking, the sharp heights of ice, had seldom been visible while they crossed the plain, snowclouds hiding all but the blue foothills. They were in those foothills now, a haven between the windy plain and the stormy peaks. They had entered a narrow stream valley which wound and widened till it opened out on the broad, deep gorge of the Grayrock. The valley floor was forested, mostly with ringtrees and a few thick stands of cottonwools, but there were many glades and clearings among the trees. The hills on the north side of the valley were steep and craggy, sheltering the valley and the lower, open, southern slopes. It was a pleasant place. They had all felt at ease there, putting up their shelters, the first day. But in the morning the glades were white, and under the ringtrees, though the bronze foliage had kept the light snow off, every stone and leaf of withered grass sparkled with thick frost. The people huddled up to the fires to thaw out before they could go gather more firewood.

"Brushwood shelters aren't what we need in this kind of weather," Andre said gloomily, rubbing his stiff, chapped hands. "Ow, ow, ow, I'm cold."

"It's clearing off," Luz said, looking up through a broad gap in the trees, where their side-valley opened out into the river gorge; above the steep farther shore of the Grayrock, the Eastern Range glittered hugely, dark blue and white.

"For now. It'll snow again."

Andre looked frail, hunched there by the fire that burned almost invisible in the fresh morning sunlight: frail, cold, discouraged. Luz, much rested by the day without walking, felt a freshness of spirit like the morning light; she felt a great love for Andre, the patient, anxious man. She squatted down beside him by the fire, and patted his shoulder. "This is a good place, isn't it," she said.

He nodded, hunched up, still rubbing his sore, red hands.

"Andre."

He grunted.

"Maybe we should be building cabins, not shelters."

"Here?"

"It's a good place. . . ."

He looked around at the high red trees, the stream rushing loudly down toward the Grayrock, the sunlit, open slopes to the south, the great blue heights eastward. "It's all right," he said grudgingly. "Plenty of wood and water, anyhow. Fish, coneys, we could last out the winter here."

"Maybe we should? While there's time to put up cabins?"

Hunched up, his arms hanging between his knees, Andre mechanically rubbed his hands. She watched him, her hand still on his shoulder.

"It would suit me," he said at last.

"If we've come far enough . . ."

"We'll have to get everybody together, agree. . . ." He looked at her; he put his arm up around her shoulders. They squatted side by side, linked, rocking a little on their heels, close to the quivering half-seen fire. "I've had enough running," he said. "Have you?"

She nodded.

"I don't know. I wonder . . ."

"What?"

Andre stared at the sunlit fire, his face, drawn and weatherbeaten, flushed by the heat.

"They say when you're lost, really lost, you always go in a circle," he said. "You come back to where you started from. Only you don't always recognize it."

"This isn't the City," Luz said. "Nor the Town."

"No. Not yet."

"Not ever," she said, her brows drawn down straight and harsh. "This is a new place, Andre. A beginning place."

"God willing."

"I don't know what God wants." She put out her free hand and scratched up a little of the damp, half-frozen earth, and squeezed it in her palm. "That's God," she said, opening her hand on the half-molded sphere of black dirt. "That's me. And you. And the others. And the mountains. We're all . . . it's all one circle."

"You've lost me, Luz."

"I don't know what I'm talking about. I want to stay here, Andre."

"Then I expect we will," Andre said, and thumped

her between the shoulders. "Would we ever have started, I wonder, if it hadn't been for you?"

"Oh, don't say that, Andre—"

"Why not? It's the truth."

"I have enough on my conscience without that. I have— If I—"

"This is a new place, Luz," he said very gently. "The names are new here." She saw there were tears in his eyes. "This is where we build the world," he said, "out of mud."

Eleven-year-old Asher came toward Luz, who was down on the bank of the Grayrock gathering fresh-water mussels from the icy, weed-fringed rocks of a backwater. "Luz," he said when he was near enough not to have to speak loudly. "Look."

She was glad to straighten up and get her hands out of the bitter cold of the water. "What have you got there?"

"Look," the boy said in a whisper, holding out his open hand. On the palm sat a little creature like a shadow-colored toad with wings. Three gold pinhead eyes stared unwinking, one at Asher, two at Luz.

"A wotsit."

"I never saw one close up before."

"He came to me. I was coming down here with the baskets, and he flew into one, and I put out my hand and he got onto it."

"Would he come to me?"

"I don't know. Hold out your hand."

She put her hand beside Asher's. The wotsit trembled and for a moment blurred into a mere vibration of fronds or feathers; then, with a hop or flight too quick for the eye to follow, it transferred itself to Luz's palm, and she felt the grip of six warm, tiny, wiry feet.

"O you are beautiful," she said softly to the creature, "you are beautiful. And I could kill you, but I couldn't keep you, not even hold you. . . ."

"If you put them in a cage, they die," the child said.

"I know," Luz said.

The wotsit was now turning blue, the pure, azure blue of the sky between the peaks of the Eastern Range on days, like this day, of winter sunlight. The three gold pinhead eyes glittered. The wings, bright and translucent, shot out, startling Luz; her hand's slight movement launched the little creature on its upward glide, out over the breadth of the river, eastward, like a fleck of mica on the wind.

She and Asher filled the baskets with the heavy, bearded, black mussel shells, and trudged back up the pathway to the settlement.

"Southwind!" Asher cried, tugging his heavy basket along, "Southwind! There's wotsits here! One came to me!"

"Of course there are," Southwind said, trotting down the path to help them with their load. "What a lot you got! Oh, Luz, your poor hands, come on, the cabin's warm, Sasha brought a new load of wood in on the cart. Did you think there wouldn't be wotsits here? We're not that far from home!"

The cabins—nine so far, three more half-built—stood on the south bank of the stream where it widened out into a pool under the branches of a giant single ringtree. They took their water from the little falls at the head of the pool, bathed and washed at the foot of it where it narrowed before its long plunge down to the Grayrock. They called the settlement Heron, or Heron Pool, for the pair of gray creatures who lived on the farther shore of the stream, untroubled by the presence of the human beings, the smoke of their fires, the noise of their work, their coming and going, the sound of their voices. Elegant, long-legged, silent, the herons went about their own business of food gathering on the other side of the wide, dark pool; sometimes they paused in the shallows to gaze at the people with clear, quiet, colorless eyes. Sometimes, on still cold evenings before snow, they danced. As Luz and Southwind and the child turned aside toward their cabin, Luz saw the herons standing near the roots of the great tree, one poised to watch them, the other with its narrow head turned back as it gazed into the forest. "They'll dance tonight," she said, under her breath; and she stopped a moment, standing with her heavy load on the path, still as the herons; then went on.

ABOUT THE AUTHOR

A resident of Portland, Oregon, URSULA K. LE GUIN was born in California, graduated from Radcliffe and earned her master's degree at Columbia University. One of the most distinguished authors of our time and winner of numerous awards, including the National Book Award, the Nebula and the Hugo, she has written many novels and short stories. Among her best known books are *The Left Hand of Darkness, The Dispossessed* and *The Earthsea Trilogy.*

WEST
of
EDEN

by
Harry Harrison

OUT OF THIS WORLD!

That's the only way to describe Bantam's great series of science fiction classics. These space-age thrillers are filled with terror, fancy and adventure and written by America's most renowned writers of science fiction. Welcome to outer space and have a good trip!

SPECIAL MONEY SAVING OFFER

Now you can have an up-to-date listing of Bantam's hundreds of titles plus take advantage of our unique and exciting bonus book offer. A special offer which gives you the opportunity to purchase a Bantam book for only 50¢. Here's how!

By ordering any five books at the regular price per order, you can also choose any other single book listed (up to a $4.95 value) for just 50¢. Some restrictions do apply, but for further details why not send for Bantam's listing of titles today!

Just send us your name and address plus 50¢ to defray the postage and handling costs.

BANTAM BOOKS, INC.
Dept. FC, 414 East Golf Road, Des Plaines, Ill 60016

Mr./Mrs./Miss/Ms. _____
(please print)

Address _____

City_____ State_____ Zip_____

FC—3/84